BOOK
OF
MERCY

BOOK
OF
MERCY

A Novel by
SHERRY ROBERTS

Osmyrrah Publishing
St. Paul, Minnesota 55124
www.osmyrrahpublishing.com
info@osmyrrahpublishing.com

ISBN: 978-0-9638880-4-4

Printed in the United States of America

CHAPTER 1

BETTER THAN BAMBI

MOST WOMEN DON'T LEARN they're pregnant and then drive for fifteen hours trying to outrun the idea. Antigone Brown did. Today the open road called to her like a siren. It whispered: Today's your birthday. You're thirty years old. And you're going to have a baby. What if she's just like you?

Much to her husband's despair, Antigone unwound on curving country roads, unraveling problems as yellow lines disappeared in the rearview mirror. Normally, the road healed. Her stress melted into the hot asphalt like ice cream. Her fears receded.

Not this time. This trip the pressure inside her had built with each passing mile. She drove through the warm night, hair flying, radio blaring, with the top down on the convertible, until she could drive no more. Finally, she whipped into a roadside park, with a spray of gravel, and braked in front of a pay telephone. She switched off the motor.

With an exasperated sweep of her hand, Antigone flung to the floor the bewildering assortment of documents from her doctor—prescriptions for vitamins, orders for lab work, handouts on prenatal care. They made her want to scream. So she did. Convertibles were perfect for a good scream. Her voice abruptly silenced the early morning twittering of the birds, but a few moments later, they were back at it again, conversing about the spring day, worms, whatever the talk was at their breakfast tables. As it grew lighter, she looked around and was struck by her aloneness. There was a single picnic table tucked back in a copse of maples. And that was it. Two-lane road, no traffic, no farms in sight. Just her and the birds.

Antigone staggered from the car, leaving the door ajar, ran to the edge of the road, and peered up at a road sign. As she slowly sounded out the words, she remembered: the smell of the girls' school bathroom. She was huddled on the cold tile floor, hiding, rocking, reciting the alphabet song over and over again. "A-B-C-D-E-F-G . . ."

"I'm falling to pieces right here on the side of the road," she grumbled. The mischievous letters on the sign continued to jump around, leapfrogging over each other. Maybe, she thought, crazy baby hormones had short-circuited her. All the little things she, a woman with dyslexia, did to cheat chaos, like singing the alphabet song, weren't working. How would she survive without her normal tricks? She rubbed her eyes and whispered, "No alphabet songs for my baby. Please."

She needed Sam.

Abruptly, she turned and headed for the telephone kiosk, old and abandoned. Without even looking at the buttons, Antigone punched in the numbers. No dial tone. She slammed the receiver down and redialed. Nothing again. She banged on the side of the phone box with the receiver.

"You need to put in some money."

Antigone whirled and squinted into the dusky light. At last, she saw a figure lying on the lone picnic table.

"Of course." Antigone dug in her pockets, but they were empty except for pellets of deer food and the small green stone she always kept in her left pocket. She glanced at the picnic table. "Do you have any money?"

"Do I look like an ATM?"

She searched her pockets again. This was the kind of thing that made Sam crazy: his wife on a lonely road, no cell phone, talking to strangers.

"Maybe there's some change in your car," the stranger yawned.

"Good thinking," she said.

"Don't mention it."

Antigone ran to the car, flung her sunglasses on the dash, dropped to her knees, and pushed her fingers in the space between the Mustang's seats. She knew the contents of her wallet: one twenty-dollar bill and a credit card. She never carried change. If you carried change, that meant, eventually, you'd have to count change, which was not an option. That left whatever the floor and seat cushions would give up. She found a barrette, some M&M candies, more pellets, and several quarters.

"Aha!" She held up the coins to the light with her dusty fingers and popped the stale, chipped M&Ms in her mouth.

Sam answered on the first ring. "Antigone?"

"Sam."

Her husband's voice instantly became alert. "What's wrong? Where are you?"

"I don't know. New York, I think."

"New York," confirmed the voice from the picnic table.

"Definitely New York," said Antigone.

"Is there someone with you?" Sam asked.

"No." Antigone shook her head, suddenly confused. "Yes. It doesn't matter."

"You're not making sense." She heard Sam sigh. "Dammit. You know how I hate this."

Antigone leaned against the kiosk, exhausted. "I know . . . but I *did* leave a message on the answering machine." Before driving north out of Mercy, North Carolina, Antigone had called home from the doctor's office—"It's official. We're having a baby. Gone for a drive. Don't worry." Antigone never left notes; she always called the answering machine, especially when she was avoiding Sam. The answering machine was the first thing he checked when he walked into the house.

"Yeah, nothing like getting one of the most important messages of your life from a damn machine," Sam growled.

"Sorry. I tried *not* to run. I really did."

"I called the doctor's office, but they said you'd already left."

"I just freaked. The doctor gave me homework—all these papers to fill out—and you know how I am with forms."

"I know, you'd rather be put on the rack," Sam said.

"I was driving around, and everywhere I looked there were babies."

"If you'd driven straight home . . ."

She lowered her head and turned her back to the figure on the table. "And then I started worrying about who was going to help our baby with her homework."

Sam's voice softened. "Tigg, why do you put yourself through this?"

"I'm going to be a worthless mother, Sam. She's going to hate me. She deserves a mother who can read."

"You *can* read," he insisted.

"But it's so hard and it takes so long. I feel like an idiot," Antigone said.

"She won't hate you."

"But the homework . . ."

"I'll handle the homework; you'll teach her to drive."

Antigone smiled at that. She wished more than anything that she were cuddled next to Sam. Sometimes, at night, she watched Sam sleep, his hard chest rising and falling with each steady breath. Even in sleep, he exuded confidence. He made her feel safe. He never needed the alphabet song.

"I'm so tired, Sam. I can't remember being this tired on other drives."

SHERRY ROBERTS

"You're killing me, Tigg. You know that, don't you? Absolutely killing me."

"Sorry."

"I tried your cell."

She kicked at a tuft of grass with the toe of her hiking boot. "I sort of misplaced it—again."

"I know. I heard it ringing. In the yard. With the deer."

Silence. She leaned closer to the phone, "Forget the phone. I just wanted to hear your voice."

Sam groaned. "William baked a birthday cake like you wouldn't believe. Quadruple chocolate. Come home, Tigg. I'm going nuts around here without you."

"I love it when you turn all sweet and mushy."

"I am never mushy."

"Sam . . ." Antigone paused, and she could almost feel Sam tense.

"What?"

Playing with the phone cord, she whispered into the receiver, "I wish you could come get me."

It was the first time she'd ever asked.

Silence, then finally, "You know I'd never find you."

What a fine pair they were, Antigone thought, the directionally challenged Sam got lost crossing the road and she couldn't even navigate her way through a prenatal brochure. What chance did their child have of being remotely normal? "Who ever heard of a mechanic who gets lost the minute he leaves the driveway?"

"This isn't my fault, Antigone." His voice was growing louder. "You're the one who takes off for God knows where

6

without a word. You jump in that little Mustang and drive until you're exhausted." Antigone moved the phone slightly away from her ear. From the corner of her eye, she saw the figure on the picnic table stir.

"Then you call me. You're a binge driver, Tigg. You get upset or stressed, and you hit the road. It's been fifteen hours! Fifteen hours is a heck of a long time when you're waiting for someone."

Antigone was swamped with guilt. She'd put him through this—again. What kind of person does that to the people she loves? She closed her eyes and imagined a happy Sam in the garage he loved, munching on Froot Loops, his comfort food, and lying under a car twirling wrenches as if they were batons. This had been a mistake. She should have gone to Sam—instead of the open road—to chase her fears away.

"Tigg, come home," Sam said. "I want to hold you and my baby. Forget about the forms. Forget everything. We'll work it all out. Like we always do."

So, Antigone decided to go home. She told Sam to get some more sleep and hung up.

She did not tell him that, for the first time on her many road trips, she was lost.

Ordinarily, Antigone found her way home without navigational aids, an ability that was incomprehensible to Sam. He lived or died by his GPS. She thought of her phone at home, with the GPS she never used. She trusted her own inner compass more than technology. Even as a child, she'd known when her mother took a wrong turn or her father was driving in circles.

But today when she searched her instincts, all she came up with was confusion. She nervously fingered the green stone in her pocket. Sam and the O. Henry Deer Farm and Café seemed so far away. William's heavenly chocolate cake sounded so good. She needed to consult a map. And she hated maps as much as Sam did. Antigone rubbed her forehead.

"You all right?" asked the voice from the picnic table.

Antigone jerked. Her head came up. While Antigone made a mess of reading anything from road signs to recipes, she was a genius at listening. It was almost an animal ability. While her deer smelled change in the wind, she heard it in the human voice. She listened to the radio, to voices from Alaska and Texas and New Zealand, and it was as if they were talking to her heart-to-heart.

The voice from the picnic table was young and tough but curious. It was not a trusting voice. Still, and this is what intrigued Antigone, there was a breath of concern.

The body attached to the voice moved. Legs swung around; a long, lanky torso sat up; arms stretched. Antigone froze, watching. A semi thundered down the road, pulling a tail of leaves into the vacuum behind it. There were no other cars at the little roadside park. Without taking her gaze from the stranger, she began edging toward the Mustang.

"Man, I'm hungry," the voice mumbled.

Antigone stopped. She stared at the figure, which was going through all kinds of early-morning rubbings and twitchings. He drilled into his eyes with both fists. She smiled. He reminded her of a boy in one of the books her mother had read to her when she was a child, some sleepy towhead in baggy jammies shaking off moon dust. It was a ludicrous comparison. Sitting on top of the picnic table, his feet in gigantic unlaced tennis shoes resting on the bench, was a black kid in thin jeans and a navy blue hoodie. He was skinny and strange and scroungy-looking. A leaf stuck to his hair like Velcro. But when he dropped his hands and looked at her, she caught her breath. It was like looking into the eyes of one of her deer. Such amazing liquid brown eyes.

Antigone's stomach growled. "I'm hungry, too," she said.

The boy shrugged. "It's a morning thing."

Because she was tired and lonely, because the kid probably hadn't eaten in days, and because *someone* was going to have to read a road map, she asked, "Do you want to get some breakfast? I'll buy."

The boy turned to stone. Suddenly, he was alert and suspicious. His stare zeroed in on her like a missile system. He slowly rose and stepped off the picnic table. She realized, with some trepidation, he was as tall as she, probably five-seven or eight. If it came to a tussle, they weighed about the same. But she figured his life experience would tip the scales. After all, he was out in the middle of nowhere, alone, obviously not afraid of her. Probably running from something. A gang? The law? Maybe breakfast wasn't a good idea.

"Are you nuts?" the boy hissed. There—she heard it again, a softness, a caring. She relaxed. He paced several feet away, turned, and paced back. He stood in front of her, fists clenched on slim hips, legs apart and locked. "Are you crazy? Pickin' up strangers. A white woman invitin' a black kid into her car. I could rape ya, kill ya, and steal your car."

"Do you know how to drive?"

The boy stared at Antigone with disbelief. He muttered to himself, "Save me from white people. They got no sense. They all livin' in Disneyland."

"You can earn your keep. Keep me awake. Talk to me." Antigone scrubbed her face. She was feeling shaky, weary. She didn't want to be alone. And her instincts told her she could trust this boy.

"I don't talk."

Antigone raised one eyebrow. "Ever?"

"Besides how you know I'm goin' where you're goin'?"

Antigone turned away and waved her hand. "Forget it. It was just breakfast; that's all. No big deal."

She slid into the front seat and slammed the door. She felt flattened. She didn't even reach for the key in the ignition. She simply draped her arms on the steering wheel and rested her head.

"You gonna sleep or we gonna eat?"

She tilted her head and watched the boy pull the car door open. He gingerly pushed aside the papers on the floor with his toe and lighted on the passenger seat like a bird. She didn't move. After a few moments, he relaxed into the seat. He flung an elbow out the window with the nonchalance of male youth and gave her a stern look. "No more screamin'."

She nodded.

"And I ain't drivin' no car. Some cop catch me in a ride like this with a white chick—." He shook his head. "That's the last anybody gonna see of old Ryder."

"Okay, Ryder." Antigone started the engine, plucked her

sunglasses from the dash, and slid them on her nose. "I'm Antigone, by the way."

His forehead wrinkled. "What kinda name is that?"

"Antigone was a girl in Greek mythology."

"Did she have a unicorn? I heard all those Greek chicks had unicorns."

"No unicorn. But I *do* have deer."

Ryder shifted in the seat and turned toward her. It was like watching one of the deer coming to attention, swirling its ears in the direction of interest. "Deer," he said slowly. "Like Bambi?"

"Better than Bambi." Antigone laughed and reached for the glove compartment.

The boy jumped to avoid contact.

In the even voice she used with the deer, Antigone said, "Just getting the map."

She unfolded the map, propped it against the steering wheel, and stared at it in confusion.

After a few moments, Ryder said, "Uh, you know you've got it upside down, right?"

Antigone rotated the map. "Sure, just getting a different perspective." The boy gave her a skeptical look. More moments passed with her studying the map and him studying her.

Ryder cleared his throat. "You expect those eggs to come to us?"

Antigone turned, edged the sunglasses down, and peered over the top at her new navigator. "Okay, Mr. Bigshot Map Expert." She shoved the map at him. "You find the nearest restaurant."

Ryder checked the road sign Antigone had been unable to read, traced one road then another on the map with his finger, and announced, "Left."

Antigone patted the stone in her pocket to make sure she turned in the correct direction and pulled out of the parking lot.

AT THE TRUCK STOP, Ryder glared at the fat truckers stuffing their faces with greasy hash browns. The pretty woman sitting across from him was attracting way too much attention. He sat straighter, junkyard dog alert, staring down anyone who even thought of approaching. They were in a booth by the window—her idea, not his. The waitress took his plate, cleaned as if he'd licked it, and delivered the bill with a frown. "Just put it on the table," Ryder said softly. She glanced at Antigone and then slid the check on the table. When Ryder continued to stare at her, the waitress harrumphed and swished away, swinging her polyester hips.

His eyes went back to Antigone. He studied the woman, arm propping up her head, snoring into a plate of cold scrambled eggs. There were shadows under her eyes, which he remembered were green-brown. She'd bunched her streaky blonde hair up in a half-ponytail, half-bun, one of those weird styles girls accomplished with a twist of the hand. Her fingers were slender, but her nails were short, no polish.

She'd tossed her wallet and keys on the table between them. He could slide them over his way without anyone being the wiser.

Instead, he sat there, for hours—watching over her.

CHAPTER 2

THE BAN OF
THE MONTH CLUB

THE APRIL MEETING OF the Mercy Study Club convened in Irene Crump's solarium, a room ablaze with rich sunlight, understated elegance, and female resolve. Here seventeen women—dressed in silk designer suits and heels—changed lives. This room, with its ceiling fans stirring air while manicured hands stirred gold spoons in demitasse cups, was command central.

The Study Club was a book club, a support group, and a force to be reckoned with. While their husbands struck deals over lunch in clubs still dominated by white males, their wives held on fiercely to their own pockets of power. When the need arose, these hothouse blooms could shake loose an amazing amount of cash and clout. They got what they wanted without breaking a sweat, raising a voice, chipping a fingernail, or bothering with official channels. Mercy was a one-industry North Carolina town of less than five thousand in danger of shrinking into oblivion. The textile mill was taking a beating from imports.

The Study Club's projects were invaluable to the community—the removal of asbestos in the high school; the fire department's new hoses and uniforms; monthly contributions of canned goods to the local food bank. Any member could bring a need to the group. A majority vote determined action.

On this unusually warm day, with the sun cooking the Jaguars, Mercedes, and SUVs parked outside her house, Irene was coolly determined. She was club president, program chair, and commander in chief. With a jerk on her silk jacket hem and an unconscious straightening of her spine (an action hot-wired into her body by a mother obsessed with posture), Irene brought the group to order. "I've been volunteering two mornings each week at the high school library. And it has been quite an eye opener. Librarian Nancy Sandhart has her hands full. The attitudes of today's youth are appalling, and as we all know, Nancy is not exactly a dominant personality. In short, I found the library itself lacking in control and its contents nothing short of questionable."

Irene upended a Nieman Marcus shopping bag and poured books onto the ornate tile floor her contractor husband Arthur had special ordered from Italy. The befuddled members of the Study Club stared at the mound of literature. They were familiar with many of the books;

some like Faulkner and Twain had been around when they were in high school. Other books such as the *Harry Potter* series looked new and were favorites of their children and grandchildren.

Irene nudged the pile with the toe of her black Prada. "Our children have complete and unrestricted access to this filth. Nancy makes no attempt to guide the young and impressionable toward more appropriate reading. She says she's too busy."

"Nancy buys these *things*?" asked seventy-six-year-old Arabella Richey, wrinkling her nose with distaste at a book about the adventures of a character called Captain Underpants. Arabella, wife of the bank president, was a mystery junkie and not ashamed to admit it.

"Apparently, they come out of the library's budget. Many were requested."

"People *asked* for this?" Arabella poked the underpants book with her cane.

"The children did." Irene swept her hand across the pile. "In effect, ladies, *we* paid for them. *This* is our tax dollars at work."

Several members looked at the heap in consternation.

"How can you be sure they're all filth?" asked a soft voice. Irene turned to Julie Masterson Clark, a thirty-five-year-old who sneaked romances into her shopping cart at the grocery store. Their daughters were on the same soccer team. Julie's grandmother founded the Mercy Study Club in 1919 as a place "where women of intelligence and culture could shine, keep abreast of the events of the day, and exercise their minds." Julie's mother had been a past president and a respected member until her death five years ago.

"Have you read any of them?" Julie asked.

"I've *perused* all of them," Irene snapped. "I also consulted some librarians I know in other towns. And I found tons of information on the Internet. I even read some of those blogs. Most of those people are idiots, but a few were insightful."

"Obviously, you've done your research, Irene, as usual," said Arabella, popping a petit four into her mouth, whole. The woman was scrawny, not a muscle left in her pampered body, but she could pack away French pastry like a sumo wrestler.

Irene balanced a pair of half-moon reading glasses on her nose and opened a dainty and expensive leather journal. In it was a nutshell description of every book in the pile. As she read the description of a book, she roamed the room, pulling books from the pile and tossing them at the feet of the members. Members scooted away as waves of "filth" edged closer and closer to their well-shod toes.

"*The Stupids Step Out,*" Irene said. "Describes families in a derogatory manner and might encourage children to disobey their parents."

Arabella huffed in disgust. "That's an absurd name for a family, fictional or otherwise. What if Tolstoy had called her Anna Idiot instead of Anna Karenina?"

Arabella got no argument from Irene, who constantly fought the battle for eloquent language with her own children. She thought "suck" should be something you did with a straw, not a description of your homework. She continued, "*Forever* by Judy Blume. Contains profanity, sexual situations, and themes that allegedly encourage disrespectful behavior . . . Personally, I don't want my daughter reading any of Blume's books.

"*Fahrenheit 451* by Ray Bradbury. One California library gave students copies of the book with all the 'hells' and 'damns', pardon my French, blacked out."

"Not a bad idea, if you ask me," said one member.

"I agree," Irene said then went on to the next book. "*A Light in the Attic* by Shel Silverstein. Encourages children to break dishes so they won't have to dry them . . ."

Irene paused for dramatic effect, watching the other members of the Study Club shift uncomfortably in their seats. She was a forty-five-year-old woman married for twenty years to a man who liked to get his way. She was also the mother of a sixteen-year-old son who thought he was smarter than she and a seven-year-old daughter, who, like her father, tended to bulldoze her way to her desires. In a family of power brokers, Irene had learned the value of controlled silence.

Julie cleared her throat and attempted a half-hearted smile. "Irene, surely when you were a child, you too hated doing the dishes."

Irene peered over her glasses at Julie. "We had a maid for that. Even so, there is never an excuse to take a hammer to the Wedgewood."

Julie looked to the others for help. Several members refused to meet her gaze. "But, Irene, some of these are classics—Faulkner, Steinbeck, Twain."

Irene shoved William Faulkner's *As I Lay Dying* under Julie's nose. "Masturbation and abortion."

She pushed John Steinbeck's *Grapes of Wrath* toward Julie. "Takes the name of the Lord in vain. Repeatedly."

At Mark Twain's *Huckleberry Finn*, Irene sighed. "Where do I start? It's a challenge magnet. I think they ought to replace the N-word with the word slaves, just like that professor suggested."

Mary Sue Hampton, a mother of five who refused to allow even her three-year-old to interrupt her afternoon reading time, sliced the tension in the room. "What is it you think we should do, Irene?" Forty-year-old Mary Sue was known to take a scalpel straight to the heart of a situation. She had time management down to a science. She made schedules of piano recitals, ballet lessons, and soccer games on her personal laptop computer, printed out copies, and posted them weekly in the kitchen, bathroom, and children's rooms. She was a born CEO and could easily have taken over her father's successful textile business.

Irene sat, tugged at the hem of her already neat jacket, and crossed her long, slim legs. Patting her hair, which was never mussed, she announced: "I think we have to ban." A soft gasp went up from the group. "Remove them from circulation—permanently. At the very least, they should be weeded from general circulation and stored safely on reserved shelves. Where they can be controlled."

"You mean checked out only with parental permission," Julie said.

Mary Sue pressed her lips together in thought. "This is a serious action."

"This is a serious issue," Irene retorted.

Julie stuttered, "This-this is censorship."

"Pornography is judged by the standards of the community," Irene reasoned. "And *we* are the community. We set the standards. If your mother were alive today, she would agree with me."

Julie reared back, as if slapped. Irene personally believed that the Masterson family gene pool had gotten watered down when it came to Julie. Irene wanted to shake her and scream: "Snap out of it. You come from doers not whiners."

Arabella huffed. "I agree with Irene. As it says in Proverbs, 'Train a child in the way he should go, and when he is old, he will not turn from it.' My goodness, we can't have children running around with primers on how to cast spells and make babies. I won't allow those *Potter* books in my house, and I had to take a Harlequin away from my thirteen-year-old granddaughter the other day. Thirteen and already a head full of sex. Things are getting out of hand."

Irene turned to Julie as if to say, "See?" and was surprised to find Julie had recovered. Her chin was lifted, and there was something close to determination in her eyes. Maybe there was a streak of her mother in her after all. "My mother would *never* have climbed on this bandwagon." She stared down Irene. "She knew when something smelled rotten, just as I do. Whatever happened to free speech? Americans don't censor."

"We don't torture either," Irene said. "But sometimes there are bigger issues at stake."

"A bigger issue than freedom?" Julie exclaimed. "We protect speech so people can get the information they need to make decisions, so they can participate in change, so they can have a say in their own lives."

"So, you put the rights of some sleazy pornographer over protecting your own children," Irene said.

Julie's mouth snapped shut. Then she turned pleading eyes to the group. "Of course not, but . . ."

"Then you agree we have to control offensive literature," Irene said.

"No."

Irene flung up her hands. "Then which is it, Julie? Make up your mind."

Julie seemed to shrink in her seat. She studied the hands clasped tightly in her lap.

Sensing victory, Irene leaned forward. "Julie, someone has to protect the children."

"Yeah," Julie muttered, "from us."

Irene sat back. She was about to launch another salvo at Julie, when Mary Sue interrupted, "Do you have a plan, Irene?"

"Of course," Irene pulled her stare away from Julie and faced Mary Sue with a smile. "It's simple. We just instruct Nancy Sandhart to take the books off the shelf."

"Just like that," Mary Sue said with skepticism.

"I *am* the president of the school board. But I think it can be done quietly—like all of our projects. I believe Nancy will be cooperative. She doesn't strike me as the type of woman eager to invite confrontation—or attention." Irene thought of the nervous woman who sneaked smokes in the women's rest room. Last year Nancy was caught smoking in

21

the teachers' lounge—four times. The principal, who had a stern policy about maintaining a tobacco-free campus and about teachers setting an example for students, warned Nancy that if he caught her smoking on school property again, she would be suspended without pay. While volunteering, Irene had learned about all of Nancy's little hiding places, the cigarettes stuffed in the back of her bottom desk drawer and stashed behind the dusty old slide projector in the supply room.

"Yes, I'm sure Nancy will be delighted to help us." Irene grinned.

Mary Sue gave a curt nod. "Then I call for a vote."

"Wait!" Julie cried. "We must discuss this . . ."

But there was no further discussion by the Mercy Study Club. Its members voted: fourteen for and three against. The motion carried. Satisfied, Irene smoothed the lapels of her jacket. "Then it's agreed. I'll contact Nancy today and give her our list."

As the Study Club filed out of Irene's spacious home, Irene closed the massive front door behind them. She leaned against the solid oak wood. Turning her eyes to the foyer's impressive cathedral ceiling, she recalled the words of her mother, who often had implied that they—the O'Connells—*might* be related to the Kennedys (another good Irish Catholic family). "The Kennedys always accepted that with great privilege came great responsibility. Something we must remember, Irene."

Irene came from governors, senators, mayors, men who would be kings in their own circles. Manners and privilege had been drilled into her. And if, while growing up, she sometimes wished she could just throw a fit, she smothered the urge. She'd been an obedient child, until she met Arthur Crump, a man with nothing who dreamed of having everything. She was swept up by Arthur's passion for life, such an unrestrained energy like she had never known. She married penniless Arthur over her parents' objections and was shocked when they cut off her inheritance.

"What will we do?" she'd cried.

But Arthur was unconcerned. He simply shrugged and whisked her away from the mansion in Raleigh to a dumpy apartment in this little town. At first, Irene thought she would die. But she survived—not that she wanted to make a habit of clawing her way out of General Store flip flops and into Pradas. She was, after all, an O'Connell, a name back in Ireland that meant strong as a wolf. She and Arthur had built their own legacy. They'd scraped and worked together, creating their own world and their own wealth.

And nothing—certainly not a few bags of filthy books or a few weak-minded women—was going to ruin it.

CHAPTER 3

INFERNO LOVE

WHILE ANTIGONE BINGED, SAM Thorne welded. The first time he'd lit the torch and cut into a 1980 Mustang was a week after their six-month anniversary. He'd known her history, how she cranked up the radio on her convertible, put it in gear, and didn't come back for days. But he thought the binge driving would end once they were married. He was wrong.

It was their first fight, he couldn't remember about what, and she went off in a huff to get a gallon of milk. She didn't come back for a whole day. Twenty-four hours of calling the police and hospitals in a panic; checking with neighbors and friends; listening to his mother's I-told-you-so's.

When Antigone returned, he wavered between being too furious to forgive and deliriously grateful that she was safe.

He marched out into the junkyard behind Sam's Garage and began dismantling cars. He pried off hubcaps, pulled off radio knobs, and dissected other parts with a torch. Then with steel and hammer and welder, he began to craft a hubcap face that resembled a Picasso woman. When he was exhausted, he turned off the welder, threw down his hammer, stood back, and assessed his first sculpture. Then he flipped the hubcap face into the field like a Frisbee, smiled, and walked away.

Now, after five years of marriage, the field behind Sam's Garage, an otherwise normal looking service station, was overrun with sculptures, a dreamy resting place for cannibalized automobiles, trucks, and motorcycles. Star, their neighbor, called Sam's sculptures his visions. But he knew the truth: they were his therapy. Every sculpture sprouting in the tall grass, every creation propped against a tree or lying beside a rusted axle was an attempt by Sam to understand his wife. It was here, among the automotive art, that he felt less alone and better able to keep himself going until her return.

In the spring rains, the ice storms, the occasional snowstorm, and the relentless Carolina summer sun, the sculptures rusted and weathered. And it seemed to Sam that the elements became a part of the sculptures. He was amazed at their ferocity, at their will to claim life from cold steel and tremendous heat. His wife was like that: a determined piece of work.

On this warm April day, Sam worked just inside the large back doors of the garage, which he'd rolled open to catch the stray breeze. Inside his protective jacket, sweat trickled down Sam's chest; it slid down his arms and into his leather gloves. He was waiting for his wife to return from parts unknown, and once again, he was controlling worry by commanding heat and steel. He fired up the welder, flipped his mask down, and pointed the welder's electrode at the joint to be joined. White-yellow sparks, appearing eerie green through the light-sensitive mask, exploded like fireworks as metal surrendered to more than three thousand degrees. The only sound was the quiet whoosh from the argon gas tank and the low sizzle of metal transforming. The perfect weld was smooth, continuous, like a stack of dimes fanned on its side. From the nozzle of the welder flowed a tiny metal wire, no bigger than pencil lead, called a bead. When he touched the wire to the joint, an electric arc was formed and the intense heat of the arc melded both the steel and the bead into one. When he pulled the wire away, the arc was broken. The sparks disappeared.

Sam lifted the mask and leaned close to examine the seam. It was a slow and hot process, putting down a bead so carefully and patiently, keeping the oxygen at bay. Oxides in a weld created bubbles, pits, or inclusions that weakened the work and would be the first place to fracture under stress. His muscles strained as he alternately hammered and welded the body frame from a wrecked Mercedes. When he was finished, no one would know that it had once been part of a luxury car. It would resemble a tornado of lowercase E's locked together, swirling out of control in a beautiful dance of alphabetic confusion. He studied the twisting shape and imagined this was how words in books looked to his dyslexic wife.

"Man, you got some weird stuff back here," said a voice

from the front of the garage. Sam jerked, catching his hand on a jagged edge of steel.

"Damn," he frowned at the cut along his thumb then glared at the stranger standing in the doorway. "You need something?"

"A fan belt, my girlfriend says. She's the mechanical one. Hell, I don't know the difference between a fan belt and a fan club."

Sam pulled a dark blue handkerchief from his back pocket and wrapped his bleeding thumb. "I'll take a look."

"Yeah, you do that, man," said the stranger, stepping through the back door and ambling toward a nearby sculpture, a bizarre map of tailpipe roads. "She'll explain the problem."

Customers. Sam shook his head. While he worked on their cars in his one-man shop, people wandered through the artistic graveyard as if they were strolling in a museum. He hated it. "One day," he'd told Antigone, "some *art lover*'s going to trip over an engine and sue us for everything we've got."

As the stranger called to his girlfriend, "Carol, you've got to see this," Sam swiped at an insect spinning about his head, which only made his thumb throb more, and marched to the front of the garage.

SAM LISTENED TO THE road. He'd pricked his ears toward Highway 74 ever since her call. He leaned into the innards of a 1983 Toyota Corolla, twisted the wrench, gripped it tighter, and yanked upward. The old spark plug had a hold like a snapping turtle's jaws. Sam wiped the sweat from his forehead with the back of his hand. A tractor-trailer whined west, and he paused. He lifted his head, craning for a hint of a familiar purr—the whisper of a motor he knew as intimately as his own face, the engine in his wife's 1968 Mustang.

The phone rang, and Sam snatched it from his pocket with a greasy hand. "Tigg?"

There was a pause. "No, it's your mother."

Sam slumped against the Toyota. He watched two kids on bikes skid to a halt by the air hose. Immediately, a hissing air war broke out. "What's up, Mom?"

"You sound . . . sad. Where's Antigone?"

"I'm not exactly sure right now."

"You mean she's off on one of her driving fits." Marian Thorne did not understand free spirits, and she most assuredly had never heard the call of the road. Good New England stock did not take flights of fancy. They were proud of feet firmly planted on the ground and believed directness was an attribute. Marian had been opposed to Sam and Antigone's marriage from the beginning. When Sam broke the news of their engagement, while sitting in the Thornes' big New Hampshire kitchen, his mother had cried, "But you're a world-class engineer. Now you want to throw it all away to work in a garage in a little podunk town in North Carolina? You have a degree from Harvard. She keeps deer as pets and sells veggie burgers and towels, for goodness sake." His mother's shoulders slumped. "Honestly, what do you two have in common? What can you possibly talk about? She doesn't think the same way we do, Sam."

That was exactly Antigone's appeal.

They'd met when he was the chief engineer on a project to replace a bridge in the next county over from Mercy. Antigone had been driving for about two days and was on her way home when her car quit, rolled to a halt not three hundred feet from the construction site. She was tired, gritty, and looked a mess. He'd never seen anything more beautiful. It was May, and she was driving the convertible with the top down. Everyone at the construction site wanted to help her, of course. A windswept blonde with a worthless car.

But Sam shouldered all the men aside and ordered them back to work. He asked a dozen questions about the car, slowly drawing out pieces of information Antigone hadn't even realized she knew, about strange sounds and knocks and behaviors that had been going on for weeks. He was a therapist for cars. While he tinkered under the hood, she fell asleep, curled up in the backseat. When she opened her eyes, several hours later, her car was fixed and he was sitting on the trunk, his work boots dangling over the edge, watching her sleep.

"You're hell on cars," he'd said. "You need your own personal mechanic."

Until he met Antigone, Sam had felt inept when it came to dealing with anything of a nonmechanical nature. Calling on girlfriends in high school, he was often sidetracked by a tricky toaster or a balky blender. This endeared him to mothers, but infuriated his dates.

The complex workings of kitchen appliances, however, couldn't compare to his wife. Life with Antigone was like standing on a new bridge in the middle of a jungle. Sam felt its strength beneath him, but he also felt a sense of vertigo, the danger of falling, rushing toward the dark Amazon water with its flesh-eating fish and rib-crushing snakes. No one could aggravate him like Antigone (especially when she disappeared for hours), but no one understood him like she did either. Only Antigone, of all the people in his life, had said, "If you don't *like* building bridges, don't build bridges."

A wife who thumbed her nose at expectations was incomprehensible to his mother. Marian Thorne had always done the expected, first as the wife of a New Hampshire judge and now in a retirement community in Florida, where she organized bridge nights and kept a vigilant eye on her husband's blood pressure.

"You know," Marian's voice grated over the telephone lines, "some women just escape into a good book or their knitting. They don't need to involve the interstate highway system."

Sam smiled to himself. Things never changed. His mother had been trying to run his life for thirty-five years. Before she could start in on some Florida property he should buy or some idea about expanding the menu at the O. Henry Café to include more reasonable food like steak, he said, "Mom, I've got big news."

"What?"

"You're going to be a grandmother."

For a moment, Marian was speechless, then he heard her shout for his father, "Jonas, we're having a baby! We're having a baby!" Marian got back on the phone. "When?"

"In nine months, I guess," Sam shrugged.

"Men. Let's see, it's late April now, and give or take a few weeks, we could have a January baby. I hope this will be an easy pregnancy. I could tell you some horror stories."

"Please don't."

"I'll send Antigone some flowers," Marian said.

"I'm sure she'd like that."

"And some baby books. There's so much to learn. Babies are not as easy as they look. They don't come with an instruction manual, you know."

"I'll read every word," Sam promised, but his mother wasn't listening.

"I do hope Antigone doesn't expose our grandchild to those wild beasts. . . ."

It was nearly midnight. Sam sat alone in the sculpture graveyard behind the garage. He willed himself to meditate, to push all thought from his mind. He must be patient and calm. He knew how it would feel the moment he saw her—as if the world had been stopped and now started again. But, for now, he must wait.

So, he closed his eyes and listened to his breathing and the highway and the voice of a barred owl somewhere. The owl's call came out of the night, a series of *hoos* that sounded like: "Who cooks for you?" It was nearby, another being reassuring him that he wasn't alone.

And while he was deliberately not thinking about her, Antigone came home. He felt her kiss on his eyelids and smelled her and, without opening his eyes, reached for her. He was sitting in the grass, his back against a sculpture that had car doors for wings. "You look like an angel," Antigone whispered, straddling his lap.

He groaned and wrapped her in his arms, hugging her even tighter. "I was worried."

"I know. I'm sorry." She kissed him again.

Sam buried his face in her hair and inhaled the distinctive scent of her. A fragrance so familiar, it even invaded his dreams at night. He thought of his child and how it would smell. New cars and babies, to Sam, were among the sweetest smells. He clamped his hand on the back of Antigone's head and nuzzled his way to her lips. He felt himself melting into her like a bead of metal. A perfect joining. A fan of dimes.

The kiss grew urgent. He pushed up her shirt with his hard, callused hands, sliding it up her soft slender sides, up, up, past her raised arms. He tossed the shirt aside and saw her grin. She reached for his shirt, and he started in on her jeans. He rammed his crazy bone into the angel wings and groaned. He closed his mouth over her breast and sucked until the pain zinging through his elbow receded and Antigone was writhing on top of him. She fumbled with his zipper. He lifted her to slide himself inside her.

What about the baby? "Should we be doing this?" he mumbled between kisses. Antigone locked her knees around his hips and sent ecstasy corkscrewing up his middle.

"Yes," she whispered, "yes, yes, yes."

He lurched and smashed his foot into the remains of a Chevy Citation.

Antigone moaned. They were like two eels twisting in a tiny space, touching everywhere. They were electrifying. Finally, they went over the edge. Two bodies glistened and arched in exquisite pleasure as moonlight shimmered over the stripped axles, bald tires, and bent automobile frames.

Across the road, the deer slept, while a wild cat prowled and stalked shadows in the night. A family of raccoons picked through the garbage behind the O. Henry Café. The barred owl hunted overhead, on the lookout for mice nesting amid the automotive ruins. Sam pulled Antigone closer, wrapping his shirt around her. They whispered in the dark, in the gallery of auto art.

"You know, you can't keep taking off without a word," Sam told her.

"Sorry. It's just that I'm so worried about her."

She already thought of the baby as a girl. He didn't care. He was just happy to have them both back in his arms. "Why?"

"I want her to feel whole and beautiful. I don't want her to feel defective or stupid. I don't want her to be like me."

Sam gulped down his temper. His wife had dyslexia, so what? It took her a while to read things, and on some days, when she was upset or stressed, she never got the words to behave. That had become his job, reading things to her: stories from the newspaper, directions on medications, instructions for the DVD player. Out of love, he kept her secret. Still, to him, her fear was irrational. People wouldn't think any less of her if they knew she had trouble reading.

"Well, that's too bad," he said. "Because I want her to

be exactly like her mother. Except for the binges. This child may not get her license until she's thirty-five."

Antigone snuggled closer. "I don't do it on purpose."

"That's not the point. I can't do this waiting anymore, Tigg. It tears me apart. I try to be strong, but . . ."

"You *are* strong."

"But it's all different now. Don't you see? I'm not just waiting for you; I'm waiting for *both* of you. I go mad just thinking of you *and* my child lost in the world."

"I'm never lost, Sam. I always find my way home."

To the navigationally impaired Sam, the idea of such complete confidence in one's directional sense was inconceivable. To him, the world was swarming with wrong turns. "Tigg, please."

Antigone took his hand. "I'll try, Sam, I promise. I'll concentrate harder." This was the automatic response of the dyslexic: increasing the effort to focus. "I just don't want to be an embarrassment to her. Mothers have to volunteer at school, read books at story hour and shit. They have to run scout troops and know all those handbooks from front to back. They have to be able to fill out forms at the hospital, school, ballet class. Childhood is one *big* form. Being a parent isn't easy."

"We'll work it out. We're going to be one big happy family," Sam said.

"Bigger than you know," Antigone said. And then she told Sam about the boy named Ryder sleeping in their spare bedroom.

CHAPTER 4

TAKING FLIGHT

STAR SIMS WAS TEN years old and the most secure kid Antigone had ever met. Maybe it was that the girl believed she was psychic and didn't hesitate to let everyone know it. Maybe it was the uncanny number of Star's predictions that came true—like the time she said a deer needed Antigone's help and Antigone found a deer, pregnant, near collapse, and cornered by three wild dogs near the back gate. Antigone ran off the dogs and rescued the deer. A few weeks later, the deer gave birth to twins.

Antigone didn't know if she believed in psychics, but she didn't *not* believe in them either. A woman with a "mystery and miracle growing inside her," as Antigone's mother described gestation, had to keep her options open.

"Have you felt the baby yet?" asked Star.

"Maybe in a few weeks," Antigone answered, glancing at the pretty child, who would someday be model tall and beautiful. Her dark hair, worn in several braids, curved around high, milk chocolate brown cheekbones. But the cheekbones were not her most arresting feature. It was those soft blue eyes, so piercingly mysterious, that nailed you. Those eyes knew secrets.

She and Antigone were sitting, resting their backs against a boulder at the edge of the pond on the O. Henry Deer Farm. They each sipped at ice teas with lemon while Fancy, a fawn born on the farm, lapped at the pond. Occasionally, Fancy glanced their way, wiggled an ear at a pesky fly, and then returned to drinking. Antigone loved the pond as much as Fancy did: the peaceful water, the tall pine trees hovering along the edges, the lazy pace. Insects floated on the surface until a frog flicked out a tongue or a fish rocketed up from the deep.

"I think it's going to be cool having a baby around," Star said. "You and Sam are going to be the best parents, I just know it."

Antigone envied the child's confidence, something she was far from feeling. She inhaled the scent of pine. Her mind, which earlier had been turning in dozens of circles within circles, was slowing. Soon it would be incapable of even a half flip. Her hands felt heavy. Her neck and shoulders could hardly support her head. She leaned back against the rock and thought of babies.

There were so many decisions to make, so many chances to do the wrong thing. Parenting was a minefield, and she felt she was wearing big clodhopper boots. Antigone realized, for the first time, how vulnerable parents were, how powerless they were in the face of love.

"It's crazy, but I already feel like I'd do anything for this baby," she said.

Star pulled her knobby knees up under her chin. "Mama says babies turn your life upside down, so it's a good thing they're cute."

Star had been firmly in that cute stage when Earthly Sims, a single mother, brought her baby daughter to town. As Antigone held Baby Star, Earthly, fresh from a divorce and desperately needing to start over, dug into a mushroom quiche at the O. Henry Café counter and talked. About leaving her job as a lawyer at the ACLU in Atlanta; about splitting from her traitorous husband, Chester, a once brilliant ACLU litigator but now corporate hack "who got too many people out of messes they didn't deserve to be gotten out of"; and about her sister who worked at the mill in Mercy.

"I'm not disillusioned," Earthly had said with a big sigh. "I'm just tired of the law, of Atlanta, of Chester. I need a break."

Antigone had inherited a nice chunk of Mercy from a never-met, never-married uncle who noted in his will that "a child with a disadvantage needs the money more than the rest of my worthless family." The bequest, on the western edge of town, included three abandoned storefronts; a long-closed restaurant named after the short story writer O. Henry; a garage, complete with a rusted hydraulic lift, broken pumps, and empty fuel tanks; a two-story farmhouse; and across the road, two hundred acres of undeveloped land.

Talking with Earthly, Antigone immediately saw the possibilities. One of the vacant storefronts stood right beside the café; Earthly had the connection at the mill to get all the seconds they wanted. Before Earthly left the café, she and Antigone had devised a plan to open a textile outlet called The Great Cover Up. As it turned out, Earthly was good at retail, and she liked managing inventory and making change, which suited her silent partner just fine. That was nearly ten years ago. Antigone had watched Star grow up.

"What do you think of Ryder?" asked Antigone.

"He's okay as strays go," Star said.

"Strays?"

"Mama says you pick up strays like us." Antigone started to deny it, but Star immediately reassured her, "Oh, it's a good thing. People need a place."

Antigone said, "I don't think of you as a stray."

"Of course not. Not now. Now we're family." Star threw her a smile.

"Yes, family," Antigone said.

Peace settled on Antigone and Star. They listened to the birds quarrel with a squirrel and chase away a hawk. They nearly slid into sleep until a ray of sun caught the reflection of an object across the pond and ricocheted the glare to their eyes.

"What's that?" Star pointed.

"What?" Antigone mumbled.

"That."

"Probably just a piece of trash."

The child rose to investigate, pushing through the waist-high foliage, and Antigone followed. As they neared the tree, Antigone's heart picked up speed. Her steps slowed.

"It's a book," Star said in amazement.

"Great, this is all I need," Antigone muttered.

The book was tucked in a place where it shouldn't have been, a crevice in the bark, not well hidden as wild things go. Reaching up, standing on tippy toes, Star tugged at the book until it came free, toppling on her head. They carried the book back and, using the boulder as a table, studied it.

Antigone traced the gold embossed letters on the brown cover with her finger and sang the alphabet song in her head. The book was old, weathered from use and the elements, with metal tips to protect its corners. It was the gold corners that had caught the sun's eye. She opened the book and, reluctantly, painstakingly, began to decipher some of the words. Sun washed over the pages, making them glaringly white; she wished she had her blue filter, a tool she used to calm the glare and make the shapes easier to discern. Still, her brain would never work like other people's. It would never reliably translate the images in front of her eyes into meaningful language. In her world of swirling serifs, everything moved.

"It's hard for you, isn't it?" Star asked.

Antigone's hands jerked. "What do you mean?"

"The words."

"There are some things people don't want others to know, Star."

"Am I being nosy?" Star pushed a tangle of braids out of her eyes and bit her lip. "Mama says I got to be careful with my gift. That I'm prone to getting into other people's business. I won't tell anyone. I promise."

Antigone studied the words on the page. She came across a "b" or was it a "d"? Her brain automatically launched one of her coping mechanisms. The "b" is shaped like a bed with a headboard, she reminded herself.

"I hate books," she said, knowing it wasn't true.

When Antigone's parents first learned that she couldn't read, they didn't believe the doctor. "What do you mean," they said, "she transposes letters? She has to unscramble words before she can read them?" This was devastating to two people who were scholars, people who lived by word and equation. Antigone's mother, Annaliese, was an international authority on the classics and ancient civilizations, and her father, Henry, was a theoretical mathematician at a small private college in Massachusetts. It was incomprehensible that a child of theirs could possess a brain wired for confusion.

Antigone's parents reacted to her disability as they did to any mathematical or academic puzzle. They read every book and journal article published on dyslexia. They looked for ways to cure, circumvent, and cope with the problem. They pressured the school to allow Antigone to take oral tests whenever possible, or at least to have the teacher read the questions aloud to her. From the beginning, Antigone had begged to be read to. She saw her parents always reading and studying, and she wanted to be a part of that world. So they read to her: children's books, classics, textbooks, academic journals. They read and discovered that once Antigone heard something, it was with her for life. Her recall ability amazed her forgetful, often distracted parents, who left a trail of Post-It notes in their wake. Annaliese, who usually cooked with her nose stuck in a book, thought nothing of peeling labels off cans in the pantry to mark her place. Antigone grew up constantly surprised by the contents of mysterious canned goods.

"One of my first memories is of my father instructing me never, under any circumstances, to write in a book," Antigone said, almost to herself.

"I got in trouble once for writing in a book," Star said. "Whew, was Mama mad."

"I think I could have robbed a convenience store, stolen a car for joyriding, and come off with a lighter sentence than if I had taken a ballpoint pen to *Babbitt*."

"What's a Babbitt?"

"A book you'll probably have to read some time."

What a disappointment she must have been to her parents, what an enigma. Antigone vowed that she would never be disappointed in her child—no matter what she could or could not do. She would teach her daughter the alphabet song, a necessity for both the dyslexic and the reader. Reading was a formidable job for Antigone. She never knew when a word, a little no-account word like "the," would send her all the way back to the start of a sentence. It seemed unfair, but Antigone had learned to live with injustice. When she was a child, she would throw down a book in disgust, crawl onto her father's lap, and burrow into his embrace. "It's so unfair," she'd cry. "It's so easy for everybody else."

Her father always replied, "Who said life was fair?"

Antigone shook off her reverie and realized that Star was staring at her. "I thought everyone liked books," Star said. "I love books."

"Why?"

"They're magic! They make me stronger and smarter. They're fun. They make me feel good."

When she was Star's age, books hadn't made Antigone feel stronger. And, books were definitely not fun. She didn't know of anything that made her feel dumber than a book.

"This is an old book," Star whispered, stroking the cover. "Sometimes old things feel like they have a life of their own. Don't you think?"

Star's words unnerved Antigone, who already believed the literary world was out to get her. She bent over the book. The words crawled toward logic and sensibility. It was a dance of frustration that she had been doing all of her life: decipher two words, stumble on one; two steps forward, one step back.

Suddenly, infuriated, she flung the book high into the air, startling Fancy the deer, which leaped into the woods. Star jumped and yelped. Antigone watched in awe as the pages spread open like wings and flapped. For a moment, she believed the book would take flight. She was shocked when it dropped into the pond and sank. Antigone gasped in horror. What would her parents think? "I've drowned a book."

But then the book popped to the surface, bobbing like a cork. A survivor. Antigone and Star looked at each other.

Antigone flung out her hand. "*That* is my life with the written word."

THAT NIGHT STAR WROTE in her diary as the pond book stood propped open on the window sill, its pages drying in the breeze. "We found the book today, just like in my vision. Poor Antigone. I wanted to tell her everything is going to be okay. But I'm not sure of that yet. I only know: this is the beginning."

CHAPTER 5

DO YOU OFFER COMBAT PAY?

"I'D MAKE A LOUSY spy," Nancy Sandhart told her good friend Antigone Brown. "The waiting, the secrecy, the deception. I'm not built for a life of subterfuge. I have a delicate system."

Nancy jumped as William placed two plates of tofu burgers and sweet potato fries in front of them. She and Antigone sat in one of the booths in the O. Henry Café. Nancy liked the café because it was book-friendly. Bookshelves marched up to the ceiling and around the door, some sagging under the weight of the books and literati litter Antigone's uncle had collected. A letter from Mark Twain complaining about his fuel bill; Flannery O'Connor's calendar; a spinner belonging to Hemingway—people said Mr. Brown was a sucker for anything allegedly literary. Personally, Nancy didn't care if they were authentic or not, and neither did Antigone.

Nancy bit into her meatless burger, dabbed at her coral pink lips with a paper napkin, and said, "Now, *you've* got what it takes."

Antigone laughed.

Nancy pointed a fry at her friend. "You've got Mata Hari nerves of steel. I know some people nearly had a fit when your uncle left you all this property." She popped the fry into her mouth. "Prime Mercy real estate. Arthur Crump was royally pissed when you refused to sell everything to him."

"Arthur *does* like to bulldoze."

"People *and* dirt. But you stood up to him. I could never have done that." Nancy was the librarian at the Mercy High School Media Center, although she preferred the word library. She believed every child who walked through the detectors at the library door was a time bomb waiting to blow up in her face.

Everyone had heard the stories: teachers being beaten, shot, or raped by grudge-holding, gun-toting, love-sick, stressed-out students. It was a violent world, and children brought it to school with them, secreted away in backpacks, pockets, and hearts.

Nancy did not like being a disciplinarian. She cringed inside every time she ejected a girl for talking too loudly or a boy for roughhousing with another student. Who knew when she'd meet them again—after school perhaps in a deserted hall or waiting by her car, tapping one of her windshield wipers, broken and bent, against the palm of a hand? Nancy would prefer a library without people.

At the counter, the boy, Ryder, was hunched over a strawberry milkshake. She hoped her friend was safe taking in such a strange child. In Nancy's opinion, there were no children who were not strange.

She eyed Ryder again. She bet he knew his way around a windshield wiper.

THE BELL OVER THE café door announced the arrival of a family of four, and Nancy's mind tumbled with thoughts: school bells, for whom the bell tolls, ding dong the wicked witch is dead. The witch, in Nancy's fantasy, looked uncannily like Irene Crump. "Irene is driving me crazy," she told Antigone.

"What's she up to now?" Antigone asked, swiping an orange fry through a puddle of ketchup. Irene often hit local businesses to support the Study Club's pet projects. Nancy knew Sam and Antigone didn't mind contributing to good causes like the fire department and the food pantry, but Antigone hated the way Irene went about it. Irene didn't ask for help; she expected it.

"Book banning."

Antigone froze before the fry reached her mouth. "Excuse me?"

"Just your ordinary, everyday censorship. And I'm her henchman, er, henchwoman."

"Explain."

"Irene's been volunteering in the library this summer. I thought it was nice of her."

"Irene is never nice."

"So I'm learning. She snooped around in closets and drawers. Found my cigarette stashes. And she was awfully curious about how we select our books. Then a few weeks ago, she came in with The List."

"The List?"

"Of books. 'The Mercy Study Club doesn't believe these books are truly suitable material for young, impressionable minds,' she told me."

"Impressionable minds," Antigone said.

"Irene strongly suggested that I pull the books from the shelves."

"You didn't."

Nancy had begun folding and refolding her napkin with the coral pink stain. "Irene can be really scary."

"What's she planning to do—burn them?"

"Oh no! I just have them stacked in a locked closet. I really thought this was going to be a onetime thing. I thought in a few weeks Irene would settle down and I could put the books back on the shelves. But yesterday she came in with another list."

"You've got to tell someone, Nance," Antigone said. "Superintendent Mitchell."

Nancy gasped. "I can't possibly. Irene will squeal on me—my cigarette stashes and the smoking in the rest room. She practically said so."

"That's blackmail."

"Irene calls it cooperation."

"She would." Antigone bit into her burger.

Nancy balled up her paper napkin, then immediately smoothed it out, only to repeat the process. She ached for a cigarette. There was no smoking in the vegetarian restaurant; Antigone said it ruined the ambiance when you were trying to push healthy choices. If they were sitting in the rocking chairs on Antigone's big wraparound porch, she could have lit up. Antigone even kept an ashtray on the porch just for Nancy.

"This is not a little thing, Nance," Antigone said softly, leaning closer. "This is real un-American, Nazi-loving censorship shit."

"Irene says it's for the good of the children, that we need to protect them."

"I think we need to protect children from people like Irene. What does Bob think about all this?" Nancy's husband Bob was a plumber, a self-employed businessman who took no guff from anyone and set his hours to fit with his passion for fishing. In the canine world, he was a basset hound married to a Chihuahua. He never got excited, while she lived in a perpetual state of angst.

"You know Bob," Nancy said. "He thinks I'm making a mountain out of molehill. He was never a big reader. Whenever I complain that working in public education is not an easy job, he says, 'So quit. You don't need that job.' He doesn't see the big picture."

"Which is?"

"I love books! This is all I ever wanted to be, Antigone.

A librarian. Working in a nice, quiet place, surrounded with the things I love. How did this all get to be so hard?"

Nancy told Antigone about an old friend, a fellow librarian in Florida. Jean Knott was Nancy Sandhart's hero. She worked in a public library where guerilla tactics were not unheard of. Jean had patrons who yelled at her, who intentionally lost books they didn't agree with in philosophy, who even returned books they found offensive half-burned and charred claiming the books accidentally fell into the barbecue as they were reading.

Antigone dropped her tofu burger. "Lord, don't tell my parents about that stuff; they'd have a stroke."

"Jean has this customer she calls Dr. Dirty Words," Nancy leaned forward and lowered her voice. "He operates on the books with a tiny knife. Jean finds little piles of words on the tables in the stacks, tiny mounds of even tinier 'hells', 'shits', 'damns', 'fucks', 'breasts', 'penises'."

"Can't she take his library card away?"

"She has. But he keeps sneaking in and she keeps throwing him out. He just waves to her with his bloody arthritic fingers—he shakes a lot and cuts himself—then drives off in an old Cadillac. He lost his driver's license years ago."

"Determined old cuss," Antigone said with a note of near admiration in her voice. She swung her legs up on the booth and eased her back against the wall. "Have you talked to Jean about Irene and her club? What does she think you ought to do?"

"She's gone through a lot of book challenges. They can be just awful, Antigone. Everybody gets mixed up in them: the patrons, the politicians, the staff. It turns the whole town upside down. Complaints. Harassment. Threats. People snubbed her on the street. She even had her tires slashed."

"Scary stuff."

"The last one was a classic, *To Kill a Mockingbird*. That went on for months. Jean lost weight and considered early retirement. She's been that town's librarian for nearly forty years. The town got a ton of publicity, which was not great for tourism. Then the ACLU arrived and threatened to make an example of the county commissioners. They quickly changed their tune and returned the book to circulation."

"So the good guys won," Antigone smiled.

Nancy wasn't so sure about that. She recalled her friend's words over the phone: "My husband said, 'Good, now life can get back to normal.' But, Nancy, it doesn't. Once you've heard their voices making threats in the night . . . So I pretend that everything is the same, that I never saw their hatred or heard their venom, that they never made me feel unsafe and afraid, that they never made me cry. Nancy, I've learned to be a diplomat, when all I ever wanted to be was a librarian."

NANCY FINISHED HER TOFU burger then vacuumed up the remains of her chocolate Malted Magi with her straw. "What if that happened here in Mercy? All that craziness and publicity and fighting. I'm not brave like you and Jean. I can't stand up to Irene and her club. I can't even stand up to a bunch of kids. I'm a nervous wreck. I can't concentrate; I can't sleep. I'm fighting with Bob over the silliest things."

Stress made Nancy feel uglier than usual. She'd begun smoking in her teens because she thought it would make her look cool, transform her from some beanpole with a long nose and stumbling feet into an elegant, sophisticated woman. In her imaginary metamorphosis, she would emerge as Audrey Hepburn in *Breakfast at Tiffany's*. So much for that. In reality, she more resembled the wet, straggly cat Holly Golightly saves in the alley in the end, an unattractive critter few people could love.

But Bob did love her, she thought, watching Antigone rub her stomach. He was a silly man, but a faithful one. And when the doctor said they'd never have children, it was Bob who shrugged his shoulders, reached for her hand, and gave her a lopsided grin.

"I shouldn't be so hard on Bob," she said.

"It's Irene you ought to kick in the ass. God, but I hate when people push other folks around just because they can."

"Irene and her friends do a lot of good for this town."

"That doesn't give her a license to run your life."

Nancy began folding and unfolding her napkin again. She *really* wanted a cigarette. "I thought maybe you could do something."

"Me?"

"You always know what to do," Nancy said. "You stand up to people all the time. Remember when the city council went berserk over the deer farm?"

"Called it a tourist trap."

"But you opened it anyway, and tourists started coming to Mercy, to the farm and the café and The Great Cover Up."

Antigone nodded. "And the world didn't end. The city council changed its mind when the tax dollars started rolling in."

"That's what I mean. You just do stuff and you don't care what they think. Like your driving. You take road trips all alone at a moment's notice. I wish I had the nerve to just drive off."

"Nance."

Nancy rushed on, pluck-pluck-plucking her ravaged napkin. "They say your uncle was like that, holding on to his little corner of Mercy, doing what he pleased. I don't know how to be that way. I don't push back very well, Antigone."

Antigone leaned over and calmed Nancy's nervous fingers with a touch of her own hand. "I'll think of something."

CHAPTER 6

WHEN WILD THINGS MEET

I<small>T WAS SO HOT</small>, Antigone said, the bees came from miles away just to suck the sweat on your arm. Ryder had never heard such a saying before, but he believed it. Every day the July sun beat down on the land in endless waves. The heat felt like a hand on Ryder's back. It woke him in the morning and followed him into his dreams at night. Tempers flared in Mercy. At the O. Henry Café and Deer Farm, mothers and fathers blew up; the slightest thing—a spilt milkshake, a whining voice, another request for money to feed the deer— could detonate their anger.

Ryder didn't wipe the sweat from his face. He stood stiffly by the mesh fence. He'd been at the O. Henry Deer Farm for nearly three months, and although he was growing accustomed to working with the deer, he still eyed the creatures with distrust. He knew the moment they sensed him. He saw the change in attitude, how their ears twitched. Their eyes calmly stared him down. He knew the routine. It was the same wherever wild things met—on the streets of New York or on a deer farm in North Carolina. Be cool and be ready to run like hell. He shrugged at the deer. The three older ones ignored him, lowering their heads, nuzzling at the grass. As usual, the two younger deer were curious. They meandered over to the fence, and Ryder involuntarily stepped back.

"They won't hurt you," said a voice behind him.

Ryder's heart jumped, the only sign that he had been caught unaware. It was Star, the girl who lived down the street. She barely came up to his chin and had legs as long and skinny as the two fawns, Noodle and Fancy. When her head moved, the blue and white beads holding her many braids jingled like wind chimes. The deer recognized the sound; they crowded closer. The girl shoved both brown hands through a rectangular opening in the fence, one of the slots used by the tourists to feed the deer. Tourists could buy handfuls of food pellets from a machine by the gate. Even though Star's hands were empty, each deer nuzzled a pink palm, and then began to lick with long, tickling tongues. Star giggled.

From the beginning, Star's smile had ambushed Ryder. It was so much like his sister Angela's. It sliced right through to his heart. He had been eleven when Angela was born, screaming and cramping, already suffering withdrawal from the drugs his mother had passed on in the womb. He knew from the beginning that Angela was his and he was hers. When he walked into the room, it was as if he turned on a light switch in Angela. Angela called for him, not their mother, at night when she woke frightened and tense, and he would hold her, listening to the sirens in the New York night, until she fell back to sleep.

Then one day, while he went out to buy bread and milk, his stoned mother watched three-year-old Angela playfully pull a plastic bag over her head. Angela suffocated. He stepped through the door of the apartment and dropped the bag of groceries. His hysterical mother was just sitting on the floor next to Angela, wringing her hands. He pushed her aside and ripped the plastic from his sister's frozen face. He tried to give Angela mouth-to-mouth liked he'd seen on TV. Nothing. He must have been doing something wrong. They didn't have a telephone so he ran across the hall, banging on the neighbor's door. "Call 9-1-1. My sister," he shouted.

Ryder blamed himself. He should never have left Angela alone with his mother that day. His self-centered mother, crazy half the time, was unable to take care of herself, much less two children. As the paramedics carried Angela from the rundown apartment, Ryder screamed at his mother. "You fucking bitch, you killed her. You're no mother; you're a worthless piece of shit. You don't care about nothin' but yourself."

He raged around the apartment, kicking a chair aside, sweeping dirty dishes off the counter. He sank onto the mattress on the floor where Angela usually slept and held his head. A few moments later, he felt his mother's presence beside him. He trembled with the need to punch her, as if hitting his mother would ease his own pain. At last, he knew how the Boyfriends felt when they looked at his weak, sniveling mother. He turned away as disgusted with himself as with her. She sobbed and begged him to stay; she needed him, she said, she only had one baby now. She plucked at his arm with desperate fingers. "God, my Angela, what am I gonna do without my Angel Baby? Lord, I need to get happy, need to take my mind off these terrible times. I have the Troubles, Ryder Baby, don't ya see?" Ryder looked into a face that could be as childlike as Angela's and as conniving as a junkie's, and shoved her hand away. That day, he walked out the apartment door and never returned.

"MAN, THERE'S SOMETHING IN the air today," Star said. "The deer can feel it."

Ryder pointed to the thunderheads gathering in the east. "Storm's comin'. Don't take ESP to see that."

Star touched his arm lightly. Like Angela, Star was a toucher. Ryder knew touchers couldn't help themselves; they had to handle the world around them. They navigated by grabbing the strings of longitude and latitude and fingering their way to global understanding. They left their fingerprints on everything. Even your soul.

Though Ryder understood touchers, it didn't make them any less pushy—or terrifying.

"Why are you so grouchy today?" Star asked. "Did you get into another fight with Sam?"

"Antigone said I could eat anything I want."

"So this is about Froot Loops."

"You eat a little cereal, and he goes ballistic." Ryder shrugged then cracked a grin. "There wasn't that much in the box to begin with."

Star looked at his pockets. Now how in the hell did she know they were stuffed with cereal? When she first introduced herself to him, she said, "My mama wanted to name me Star, but my daddy said that didn't sound very African to him. My daddy's name is Chester, and he's always wanted an African name. So they called me Kenisha Star Sims. But nobody calls me Kenisha; I'm Star. Like the star that led the wise men."

Ryder started toward the gate. "You helping today or just here to bug me?" he said. Star followed him. Once through the gate, he secured the door and double-checked the latch. That was the number one rule at the deer farm: make sure the door was latched so no dogs got in. Across a clearing, he saw Antigone starting to heft a bag of grain and hurried to help her.

"I'll get it," he said, shouldering her aside. He tossed the bag of feed into the wheelbarrow. In the months he'd been living with Antigone and Sam, his skinny arms had filled out and his muscles had grown hard from lifting feed bags, pushing the wheelbarrow over ruts and through the mud, and eating more food than he could ever imagine. He had even started to like some of the vegetarian crap William dished out over at the O. Henry Café.

He saw Antigone place a hand on her gently rounded

stomach. He'd heard her tell Sam that they were through the first trimester. He didn't know what that meant, except Antigone had stopped eating saltines in bed and upchucking her guts in the bathroom every morning. Which was fine by him. The sound of a heaving woman was not one of his favorite wake-up calls.

They fed the deer a mixture of corn and soybeans. Essentially, it was cow feed, which seemed to Ryder kind of boring. He always thought deer ate trees and stuff. He and Star filled the aluminum water bowls with a garden hose and replaced the big white blocks called salt licks.

The five white-tailed deer ignored them as Antigone and Ryder went about their duties. He knew the deer by name now and how they'd gotten here: Cleo and Lydia had both been shot by hunters. Apple had been run ragged by dogs, barely making it to the farm before birthing the twins, Noodle and Fancy, nearly a year ago. The deer farm was their sanctuary. Inside the eight-foot fence, they were safe from dogs and hunters. Between Antigone and the tourists, they got more attention than most pets. For the most part, Ryder understood the deer. Like Ryder, they had a good setup.

The one creature he didn't get, and practically nobody else did either, was the cat that had befriended the deer. The calico sauntered among them, as if it were in a still life. It lapped from the deer's water bowls and slept with them. It ignored the cat food Antigone provided. It chased chipmunks and mice, and, when it caught them, dropped the dead rodent souvenirs at the feet of one of its adopted friends. No one even considered trying to name it.

As the skies darkened, the deer grew increasingly restless. They broke into full runs without warning—and stopped just as suddenly and mysteriously. The cat slid between their frisky hooves like a shadow. The deer played tag and boxed. Ryder stared as two of the adults, each probably tipping the scales at more than a hundred pounds, reared up on hind legs and punched at each other with their front hooves. They pawed the air. Antigone walked up and laid an arm across his shoulder. Startled, Ryder tried to edge away.

"They're gonna kill each other," he whispered.

"They're just having fun." Antigone smiled. "But don't *you* get near them when they're like this."

Star nodded. "This is deer play, not people play."

Antigone said, "Those hooves are sharp and strong; they can break your arm or your nose and you won't know what hit you . . ."

The sound of a slamming gate cracked like a rifle shot in the air. Ryder, Antigone, and Star spun around. The loud clang startled them—and the deer. Sam stomped toward them, head down, obviously in a hurry. "Antigone! I've got to run out to Arthur Crump's site. Transmission problems. Need anything while I'm . . .?"

Antigone took a step toward him, hand held out. "Sam!" she cried, but before she could voice a warning, the herd scattered. All of them except one. One of the boxing deer, still pumped with adrenaline, charged, instead of fleeing—right at the cause of the disturbance. Sam's head jerked up. He froze. The boxer skidded to a halt before Sam, rose on its hind legs, and attacked. With its front hooves, it beat a tattoo on Sam's chest, a brief rat-a-tat-tat, a soft drumming by deer standards that left Sam stunned. As suddenly as the attack occurred, it ended. The deer wheeled and fled into the woods.

At first, Sam didn't move. Then he swallowed and slowly looked down at his chest. Ryder stared at Sam's chest as well. He didn't know what he expected to see—perhaps Sam's heart dangling by an artery from an opened cavity or broken ribs protruding like spears. Instead he saw hoof prints climbing up Sam's white T-shirt. That's gonna hurt like hell tomorrow, he thought.

"As I was saying," Antigone said to Ryder and Star as they approached a dazed Sam, "don't make any sudden movements or loud noises around the deer. They're gentle creatures by nature, but they still have that fight or flight instinct. And," she motioned toward Sam, "you never know which they'll choose. Always remember that as friendly and loving as they seem, they're still wild things."

As Antigone led Sam off in the direction of an ice bag and salve, Ryder cast a wary glance at the herd, which had settled and was grazing as if nothing had happened.

Star's mother called her in to practice the piano. "You be okay?" the girl asked.

He gave her an exasperated look. Star nodded then walked to the gate. After she was through and the latch secured, she sprinted for home.

The sky rumbled. He turned back to the deer. "I ain't afraid of you," he told them.

CHAPTER 7

FAST AND FURIOUS

WHILE SAM ICED HIS chest and Star practiced her piano, Antigone decided to give Ryder another driving lesson in the Mustang on the back roads around Mercy.

"You sure you can leave him?" Ryder asked, trying to get out of the lesson.

"Sam's a fast healer. He's already feeling better," she said, tossing him the keys.

Snatching the keys from the air, he reluctantly settled into the driver's seat and turned over the engine. Ryder liked to be in control, which was a word that didn't even enter his mind when he thought of cars and driving. He listened and tried to react as Antigone instructed, but, to someone who had never even ridden a bike, the car seemed way too fast and too large for this narrow country lane. Worse, the

Mustang had a mind of its own, like those hotrods from hell in the movies, the kind that sniffs out and corners humans, then runs them over—repeatedly.

"I'm barely touchin' the gas, and it's leapin' out of its skin," Ryder complained.

"Relax. You're trying to control too much."

The Professor used to tell him that, too. He and the Professor had looked out for each other on the streets of New York. They'd been a weird pair: a skittish, angry black kid and a used-up old white guy with a British accent and manners that could charm the hearts of the meanest female volunteers at the soup kitchen. "Why are you always trying to control things?" the Professor had asked Ryder once.

"So they don't control me," Ryder told him.

The Professor laughed. "You'll never be able to control it all."

"I can try."

"But, my boy, it takes but a single butterfly to do you in."

A butterfly? What's that supposed to mean?

The Professor explained how a butterfly lazily flapping its wings in China could change weather patterns in Canada. It had to do with something called the chaos theory. Chaos, Ryder snorted. That he could understand; chaos was his middle name.

"Ever hear of the chaos theory?" Ryder glanced at Antigone.

"Butterfly. Weather. Yada, yada, yada." She pointed to the windshield. "Look where you're going."

Ryder's head whipped to the front just in time to see the

large pothole ahead. The car jerked as it hit the edge of the pothole, and Ryder fought to straighten the wheels on the gravel road. "Shit. This is a waste of time. I told you I ain't got no birth certificate."

"Don't have," Antigone corrected.

Ryder scowled. "Can't get a license without a birth certificate. If my mom ever had mine, she probably rolled a joint with it and smoked it."

Antigone gave him one of her "what bullshit" looks. "I'm working on it," she said. "You're going to need it to register for school anyway."

"School?" His hand jerked, and the car jumped.

"Keep your mind on what you're doing."

Ryder battled with the touchy gas pedal of the Mustang. "Whoa. I never agreed to no school. I ain't been to school in years."

"Then it's about time you went. There's nothing to be afraid of."

"Who said I was afraid?"

"Well, you *sound* defensive."

WHENEVER RYDER HAD A driving lesson, wildlife in the vicinity went into hiding, as if word had gotten around about the squirrel he'd nearly clipped and the turtle he'd flipped into the ditch. Antigone and Ryder rode in silence. Finally, Antigone turned on the radio. Voices filled the car.

"Sam says you listen to the radio and forget to come home," Ryder said.

SHERRY ROBERTS

"It's a bad habit," Antigone admitted.

"You run away." He glanced at the woman with the flying hair.

"Not as much as I used to," she said.

Ryder arched an eyebrow at her.

"Okay. I turn on the radio to keep from thinking and then I get involved in someone else's problems. Before you know it, I'm hundreds of miles from Mercy and Sam and the deer. Sometimes I don't even know what state I'm in. It drives Sam crazy."

"You don't say," Ryder said sarcastically.

"I can't seem to help it." Antigone's voice turned thoughtful. "When I was little, I used to take the radio to bed with me. I loved hearing those voices. Talk radio. Have you ever really listened to people sometime?"

"I try not to," he said.

She ignored him. "You can hear their whole life's story in their words. You can hear if they're happy, in love, or hate their job. If they're afraid to go home at night. If they wish they'd done it all differently."

"All?"

"Life. The men they fell for, the children who hate them, the dreams they let slip away."

"You can hear all that? Damn, they all sound like loonies to me."

Antigone laughed. "You're like Sam. He doesn't believe anything he can't touch or hammer or tighten with a wrench."

"I ain't nothin' like Sam."

64

At Ryder's tone, Antigone turned in the seat. "You two are more alike than you think."

"He's always raggin' on me about eatin' his cereal and sittin' in his chair. I don't think he likes kids, especially the black variety. Are you sure he's good father material?"

"He's not like that."

"Sure, we livin' in Disneyland, and I'm Mickey Mouse."

Antigone said, "I hate it when you pull this oppressed shit."

"I *am* oppressed."

"Right now, you're just a lousy driver."

Ryder glared at Antigone. "I never asked you to teach me."

"I—" Antigone grabbed the wheel. "Watch out!"

Ryder's head snapped to the front and saw a screaming steel monster bearing down on them. The driver, a white kid, laid on the horn and defiantly held his position in the middle of the narrow road. He stuck his arm out the window and flipped them the bird. Ryder quickly jerked the wheel to the right. Bushes raked the side of the car, like scraping a chalkboard, sending shivers down his spine. The Mustang's wheels crunched through the heavy gravel that had built up on the edge of the road and started down an embankment. At the bottom of the ravine was a sturdy line of trees. "Brake!" Antigone shouted. "Stomp on it!"

Ryder stood on the brakes, and the car fishtailed to a stop just short of the trees. The quiet was immediate and loud. For a moment, they just stared out the windshield in shock. Then Ryder closed his eyes and dropped his forehead against the steering wheel. Antigone let out a shaky breath and instinctively wrapped her arm around her belly, "Shit."

"Fuck," Ryder whispered. Suddenly, his skin felt cold and sweaty. He turned toward her. "You all right?"

"Yeah. You?"

His heart had pitched down to his toes. He didn't have enough strength to swat a fly. He watched Antigone pass a hand across her face and noticed her hand was trembling. "You shouldn't be driving with me in your condition."

"No one's hurt."

Grasping the wheel 'til his knuckles turned white, teeth clenched, Ryder said, "Who the fuck was that?"

"Art Junior. Irene Crump's boy."

"He nearly killed us."

There was an edge of anger in Antigone's voice. "He's a menace, all right. I don't know what Arthur was thinking. It's insane to give a sixteen-year-old kid a vehicle with wheels big enough to crawl up walls like Spiderman. Especially that kid."

"He's an asshole," said Ryder, as a butterfly lighted on the windshield wiper.

RYDER FLAGGED DOWN A farmer heading into town. The man knew Sam and was happy to pull the Mustang back onto the road with the winch on his pickup. Ryder had feared that he'd wrecked the car, but Antigone didn't seem upset by what she termed "a few scratches."

"Easy paint job," she said. "Sam can fix it."

"Yeah, but who's going to fix me when Sam gets through with me?"

Ryder knew Sam was going to give him grief—and he didn't blame him.

He and Antigone argued over who would drive home. She pulled some crap about getting back on some horse, and he ended up reluctantly starting the engine. Back at the O. Henry Café, Star was waiting for them. She grinned at Ryder as he climbed out of the car, moving as if he were an old man. Before he could tell her what had happened, she rose from the front step of the café, dusted off the seat of her shorts, and said, "Don't worry. Art Junior's an asshole."

CHAPTER 8

INVISIBLE MAN GOES
TO SCHOOL

IT WAS THE NIGHT before the first day of school. Muggy August air slipped into the bedroom from the window. Sam rolled over in bed and rested his forehead against his wife's. He and Antigone were arguing—in whispers—so the boy down the hall wouldn't hear. She was intent upon enrolling Ryder in Mercy High School. Sam was determined to keep their irritating houseguest from flipping their family sideways.

"He should be living with his own family and going to his own school," Sam said.

"He ran away from them."

"That should be a clue right there. What's he running from? For all we know, he could be wanted for murder somewhere. After four months, we still don't know anything about him. Every time I ask him a question he accuses me of being a mechanic for the Gestapo."

"He's here. With us. Part of our family now."

"He's nothing like us. He's more man than child. He's been places and seen things we can't imagine."

Antigone shook her head. "He's working hard with the deer, and he's started helping William in the café. I think he likes it here."

"How can you be so naïve?" Sam muttered. "It's a tactic to get on your good side."

"He doesn't like being indebted."

"It's easy to be proud when you're eating another man's Froot Loops."

"Again with the cereal, Sam?" Antigone said.

"We had some ground rules when he first came. He and I had the man to man. And he breaks the rules all the time." The rules, laid down in a testosterone-charged conversation in Sam's Garage while Antigone was taking a nap, boiled down to three edicts: Keep your hands out of the Froot Loops. Don't sit in Sam's favorite TV chair. And most importantly, don't *ever* hurt Antigone.

Antigone rubbed her forehead. "I don't know what you're talking about."

"Believe me, he knows."

"Would you listen to yourself? You're supposed to be the adult."

"I don't know how in the hell I got to be the villain here. I'm a nice guy. I don't kill small animals for the fun of it; I open doors for women; I pay my taxes. I think the kid's a racist."

Antigone laughed.

"He plays the race card all the time," Sam said. "If I yell at him for sitting in my chair, he says it's because he's black. If I tell him to clean up his room, it's because he's black."

Antigone snuggled closer. "What's really on your mind?"

"I just never thought he'd stay this long. I thought we'd have this time to ourselves, you know. Planning for the baby together." Sam massaged her shoulder. "It's just weird, Tigg. People are asking about him and us, what we plan to do with him."

Antigone lifted her head and frowned at him. "What?"

"I can't change the way the world is, Antigone."

"You could tell them to mind their own business," Antigone said.

He tried to pull her back into his arms, but she resisted. "My job is to protect you and the baby," Sam said. "You can't help every underdog you meet."

But his wife believed she could. She took in strays: deer being chased by hunting dogs; Earthly Sims rebounding from a divorce with a baby in her arms; William, a sixty-year-old merchant marine with an oversized cobra tattoo slithering up his arm, a talent for vegetarian cooking, and nowhere to go; and now Ryder. Hell, Sam thought, even he was one of those strays—a logical engineer lucky enough to wander into Antigone's crazy world.

"I'm sorry you don't like it, Sam, but this is who I am. Antigone. Like in the story."

He knew his Greek mythology but listened anyway.

"Antigone was a Greek woman who lost both brothers to war. The king, Creon, honored one brother with a proper burial, but decreed that the other be left to the dogs and vultures because he fought on the opposing side. Antigone defied the king and buried the second brother. Furious, the king sentenced her to be buried alive. She hanged herself before he got the chance."

He knew it was all about family for her. He just never thought their family would look like this.

Antigone slipped an arm across his chest and pressed herself against him. "If our child were alone in the world, wouldn't you hope that someone would give her a chance?" Antigone was four months pregnant. Some days Sam caught his wife standing before the mirror, sideways, looking at the small swell of her stomach. He touched that gently rounded tummy now. Soon life would twitch beneath his fingers, and, as usual, the thought made something melt inside him.

He kissed her hair and pulled her closer. "Just don't get too attached to him."

"Are you jealous?"

Sam was, a little bit, but he refused to admit it. "He's a wild thing, Antigone. You, better than anyone, know that the wild always calls."

ANTIGONE AND RYDER WAITED in the main office of Mercy High School, shifting in a row of uncomfortable, old, creaky chairs. With each swish of the heavy door, the sounds of students chattering and lockers slamming flowed into the quiet room. Boys and girls bounced in and out of the office, delivering notes, getting papers signed, asking questions.

In a new green T-shirt that said, "Born to Be Wild," Ryder pretended boredom, when really his heart was banging like some crazy-ass drum. Last night sitting on the front porch step with Star, long after Antigone and Sam had gone to bed, he'd still been in a state of denial. He wasn't going to school. He was leaving. He didn't need this crap.

"You don't have to worry, you know," Star said.

Ryder frowned at her. "I ain't scared."

"Sure, you are," Star said breezily.

"I told Antigone she's just wastin' paper buying that new gear. I ain't even decided if I'm going for sure."

"You're going."

"Don't give me that psychic shit."

And yet here he was. He called himself all kinds of stupid. The last time he'd been in school was the ninth grade. When he began missing days to look after Angela, his mother hadn't even noticed—or cared. "I can't control the boy," she told the truant officer.

The Professor, who'd been his friend for years, took a different view. The Professor had been disappointed when, after Angela died, Ryder dropped out for good and took to the streets. "Education," the Professor used to say in his goofy hoity-toity accent, "is something they can never take away from you."

The problem was getting an education was a pain in the ass. Ryder had nothing against learning stuff; he liked books and reading, but the rest of it—the nagging teachers, the rules, the crap from other kids—that was something else.

His old school had been nothing like this one. At Mercy High, there were no walls decorated by tag artists who would paint anything that stood still, and no wire mesh over the windows to prevent students from throwing desks—or other students—out the window. Antigone told him Mercy High School was more than one hundred years old. He believed it. With big old white pillars in the front, it looked like some kind of plantation house, some place black folk should be wary of.

Antigone told him the school was about half black and half white. He wondered if that was going to be a problem. Probably, he thought, catching a glimpse of Art Junior, swaggering down the hall, the center of a pack of loud, husky boys. Art Junior spotted Ryder, said something to his buds, and made a motion like he was driving a car. Then they all burst out laughing.

Ryder shot a look at Antigone. She hadn't seen Art Junior. She was leaning back in the chair with her eyes closed. He turned back and threw Art Junior the finger. The smirk dropped from Art Junior's face, and he lunged toward the door. But just then a teacher came by, intent on clearing the halls, and Art Junior and his gang were herded off to class.

"Smart, Ryder," he said to himself. "Fucking brilliant."

He was going to hate this school, but he would give it a try. For Antigone. Because he was getting free clothes and free food and a room all to himself, something that had never happened before. Because he liked the deer and it was fun to aggravate Sam. Because, for a while, it was nice to belong somewhere.

THE SECRETARY IN THE main office called "Next!" and Ryder and Antigone both jumped to their feet. The secretary's name badge identified her as "Mrs. Sweetings, Volunteer." As a former child with special needs, Antigone was no stranger to dealing with teachers, school administrators, and well-meaning volunteers. In a glance, she had Mrs. Sweetings summed up. Everything matched on Mrs. Sweetings: big chunky gold earrings and gold bracelet, silk walking shorts and silk sweater, black tights and black leather pumps. Mrs. Sweetings probably had gone through a one-week training course. From the way she kept neatening the already neat stacks of forms in front of her, Antigone knew this was Mrs. Sweetings's first day in the main office. On the outside, she appeared calm and brave, but on the inside Antigone bet she was panicking. Antigone had heard her whisper to one of the other volunteers, "No one mentioned anything in training about boys with pierced tongues and girls with shaved heads."

Antigone relaxed for the first time since they entered the school; this woman she could handle.

"Now," Mrs. Sweetings smiled at Antigone. "What can we do for you?"

"I'm here to register a student."

Mrs. Sweetings's smile was plastered on. "No problem. Where's the student now?"

Antigone pointed to Ryder. Mrs. Sweetings's glance scanned Ryder then returned to Antigone. There was a faint flicker in her white perfect smile, a barely detectable power glitch. She asked Antigone, "And you are his . . .?"

"Aunt," Antigone smiled.

"Aunt?"

"Ryder takes after his father's side of the family."

"The father's side?"

"My sister, well, she's my stepsister really, is a single parent, and she thought it would be better for Ryder to come and live with me for a while. She was worried about what the city does to a child, the drugs and the gangs and the drive-by shootings. She naturally wants the best for her child. And I told her there was nothing better than Mercy. Don't you agree?"

Mrs. Sweetings cleared her throat. "Of course," she stammered.

"So here we are." Antigone pushed up her sleeves and grabbed a pen on the desk. "Now where do I sign?"

Mrs. Sweetings's recovery was slow. "Well, first we need a little information. If you'll fill out this form, we can get started." She handed Antigone a clipboard.

Antigone guided Ryder back to the squeaky chairs and shoved the clipboard into his hands. When he gave a quizzical look, she said, "Well, you can't expect me to do all the work."

Ryder grunted. He hated answering questions about himself. She watched him labor over the form. You'd think she had asked him to tap a vein. "Well?" she finally asked.

He read his answers. Name: *Irwin Cassius Butler. Answers to Ryder and nothing else. ABSOLUTELY NOTHING ELSE.* Age: *15.* Mother's name: *Felicia.* Father's name: *William* ("It's as good as any other," Ryder shrugged). Last school attended: *Colby Middle School, New York.* All inoculations up to date: *Yes.*

Antigone hadn't a clue how much was true. She didn't ask.

They returned the form to Mrs. Sweetings, who smiled and said, "Now if I can just make copies of your birth certificate, vaccination record, and school transcript?" Ryder looked at Mrs. Sweetings's outstretched hand, then turned to Antigone.

"Oh, we don't have any of those things," she said, with an airy wave of her hand.

For the first time, Mrs. Sweetings lost her smile. "No birth certificate?"

"Stolen by gangs when they broke into his mother's apartment looking for drug money."

"No school transcript?"

"The school burned down and all the records with it. Gangs." Antigone sighed, "Again." She gave Ryder a sad smile and a pat on the shoulder. "He lived in a very bad neighborhood."

"Sounds like a war zone," Mrs. Sweetings observed.

"That's about the size of it," Antigone said. "Is it any wonder his mother was frantic to get him out of that environment?"

"Well, what about the vaccination record?"

"We did have that," Antigone saw Mrs. Sweetings's tense shoulders begin to relax, "but my deer ate it."

"Somehow that doesn't surprise me," Mrs. Sweetings said. She shuffled the forms in front of her and restacked them in even neater piles. "Ms. Brown, I really can't admit the boy without some documentation that he even exists."

"Course, I exist. I'm standin' right in front of you," Ryder said belligerently. Mrs. Sweetings took a step back.

Antigone quickly inserted herself between the two. "Look, would just a birth certificate do?" Mrs. Sweetings gave a curt nod. "I'll have my sister write the county clerk's office in New York and get them to mail us a copy. Surely, there's one on file. In the meantime, can't he just start school?"

"I'm not supposed to do this, Ms. Brown."

"Mrs. Sweetings," Antigone appealed, "this isn't some impersonal place like New York. Don't we in Mercy care what happens to our children? This town didn't get its name for being rigid and inflexible."

It actually was named for a textile mill, where at the turn of the century children much younger than Ryder worked long hours beside their parents amid noisy and danger-ous machinery. In its heyday, Mercy towels were known throughout the country as "the bath towel that shows no mercy to moisture."

"Well," Mrs. Sweetings considered for a moment, "we wouldn't want him to get behind in his schoolwork. But I will be watching the mail for that birth certificate, Ms. Brown."

"Of course." Antigone shook her hand and thanked her.

"Simply take this form down the hall to the guidance office, and they'll help you with your schedule. Welcome to tenth grade, Irwin."

Ryder stiffened beside Antigone, who grabbed the paper and quickly ushered him out of the office. "She start spreadin' that Irwin shit around, and we're gonna have a problem," he said.

CHAPTER 9

DOING BUSINESS
WITH HECTOR BOB

"You realize we're probably breaking, like, a zillion laws," Ryder said.

Antigone looked at him. "Yeah. Don't tell Sam."

Antigone Brown, five months pregnant and enchanted with fetal kicks in the middle of the night, felt the tug of maternal instinct grow stronger with each day. Babies were like the moon, she discovered, capable of great gravitational effects on the senses and feelings of their mothers. Perhaps that's why she found herself in a deserted back street that served as the office of a man named Hector Bob. Something she didn't understand had pushed her here, and she couldn't remember ever being so frightened.

"I need to go to the bathroom," she said.

"You went five times on the way," Ryder said. "And I wouldn't trust the 'facilities' around here."

Antigone glanced around them. He was right. It was a bright September day, a day to ride with the top down and laugh and embrace the wind. Instead, they huddled in the red Mustang behind an abandoned hotel in a once bustling part of Greensboro, North Carolina. Antigone had intentionally parked in the middle of the alley, in the glaring sun, away from the shadowy buildings. Ryder complained that they were too exposed with the convertible top down, but Antigone insisted that she needed air—lots of air.

At one time, trains rattled the railroad tracks behind the old hotel. Sleepy travelers woke to shaking beds and the early morning light in their eastern windows. Now mice and vagrants slept peacefully in the abandoned clapboard hotel and traveled the unused tracks like trails through the urban woods. It was a forgotten place, left behind by glass skyscrapers, a place for rendezvous of the questionable kind.

Sam thought they were shopping for a baby stroller when, in reality, they were in the market for a birth certificate. It had taken Antigone a while to arrive at this point. First, she'd tried official channels, but there was no New York birth certificate filed for Irwin Cassius Butler.

Ryder wanted to forget the whole deal after that, but Antigone was obsessed with securing documentation of Ryder's birth. She had explained that he would need it for all sorts of identification in the future. Eventually, Ryder caved. "I might know a guy who knows a guy." That guy was Raul in New York, who understandably was cautious about doing business with a strange woman from North Carolina. But she nagged and pleaded in one telephone call after another; she was becoming quite good at badgering, just like a real mother. Finally, just to keep her from calling him anymore, Raul put her in touch with his "Southern connection," Hector Bob.

Hector Bob had been equally leery, asking numerous questions and hanging up on her several times. But Antigone kept calling, and finally, they reached the stage of negotiation. She suggested a park for their meeting; he was adamant about the location, an alley behind a rundown building in Greensboro. He preferred doing business at midnight; she told him it was Saturday, mid-morning, or no deal.

"How will I recognize you?" she asked, when they'd finally nailed down the details.

"That won't be a problem," Hector Bob said. "And bring cash."

As soon as they had entered the city, Antigone had seen the shadow of change pass over Ryder. She felt him drawing on a mantle of alertness and suspicion, a posture she hadn't seen in full bloom since they first met. She realized she had enjoyed watching Ryder relax in the months they'd been together. Some days she even saw the child in him again and felt inexplicably happy. This was city Ryder, and she hated seeing him return to that hard-shelled stranger. She wanted to hurry home, where he would become her Ryder again. Where the hell was Hector Bob?

As they sat in the sun, in the quiet warmth, Antigone thought: Mothers do crazy things for love. The mother of a Texas cheerleader once hired a hit man to eliminate her daughter's competition. Mothers starve so their children can eat. They trudge in worn-down sandals so their teenage daughters can add to their Ugg collections. Mothers will love and love and love—no matter the number of pierced body parts, forgotten birthdays, lame excuses, and silent nights waiting for phone calls. Maternal instinct is soldered onto the female soul and sometimes it just bypasses other instincts for fair play, for common sense, for survival; instincts like the one screaming inside her right now, "Get out of here!"

"This goes south, you gun it out and don't look back. Forget the damn papers," Ryder said, his eyes continuing to survey their surroundings.

Antigone tapped the steering wheel nervously. "Stop it. We do the deal, and we're out of here. We're not leaving without that birth certificate. I'm not going through this hell again."

"Sam's gonna kill me if he ever finds out I let you do this," Ryder muttered.

"You let me? I'm the one who should have her head examined, dragging a kid into this. What was I thinking? I should have dropped you off at a Starbucks to wait for me."

Ryder gave her a look that said *get real* and ignored her.

Tap, tap, tap on the steering wheel. "This is what bad mothers do. They drag kids to mysterious meetings in unsavory places with strange and probably dangerous men."

"I'm an expert on bad mothers," Ryder said. "You don't even come close to making the cut."

PRETENDING TO STARE OUT the windshield while she watched Ryder out of the corner of her eye, Antigone said, "Even though the clerk's office didn't have a birth certificate for you, they had one for your sister. Your mother gave birth to a girl named Angela. What happened to her, Ryder?"

"I don't talk about Angela," he said, slowly shifting in the seat, giving her his full attention. His eyes hardened. "She's gone. That's all you need to know."

"Sorry."

She waited.

After several long moments, he said softly, "She was sick from the beginning. We had to take her to the hospital."

"So that's why there's paperwork on her."

Ryder turned away, his arm propped on the door. "She gone, and she never coming back."

Antigone nodded and turned back to watch for Hector Bob, who was already an hour late. "Where the hell is this documentation salesman?" she grumbled. "He's probably watching us, making sure this isn't a setup."

"I would."

"I wish I knew more about this stuff," Antigone mumbled. "Everything I know about meeting people in deserted alleys I learned on TV."

Ryder groaned. "This Disneyland all over again."

Antigone stiffened. Over Ryder's shoulder, she saw what

could only be Hector Bob sauntering across the railroad tracks toward them. She caught her breath and clutched her stomach. Ryder's head whipped around. Hector Bob was lanky and tall, his ill-fitting white summer suit hanging on him in a jaunty manner. He wore no tie, just a ribbon-collar shirt buttoned up all the way to his Richard Nixon Halloween mask. He reached the car, leaned against the convertible on Ryder's side, and examined his fingernails.

"Good morning," Hector Bob said, "and Happy Halloween."

The alley just got quieter and creepier. Antigone searched the dark doorways of the abandoned buildings. Ryder edged closer to her, ready to spring if Hector Bob made a move toward her.

Antigone cleared her throat. "Hector Bob?"

"In the flesh."

"Nice mask."

"Thank you, but it's hotter than hell."

"It's a little early for trick or treating."

"What can I say? I like the holidays." Hector Bob stepped back and examined the convertible. "Sweet ride."

"Thanks," Antigone said, wishing she were anywhere but here, wishing they were tooling down some wide open road. Her insides felt like a bowl of Cream of Wheat that had been sitting too long, full of lumps.

Ryder, who wasn't one for chit-chat on a good day, interrupted. "Got the papers?"

Hector Bob patted the pocket of his suitcoat. "Got the cash?"

Antigone patted an envelope lying between the seats on the gearshift.

They exchanged envelopes, leaning across Ryder, careful not to touch fingers in passing. Hector Bob counted the money twice. Antigone took her time examining the fake birth certificate, pretending that she dealt in false credentials all the time. She was so nervous, the letters were practically vibrating. She couldn't make out a single word. She passed it to Ryder.

"What do you think?" Antigone asked.

Ryder shrugged. "Everything's spelled right. It'll fool the DMV, the school."

"It'll fool God," the documentation dealer drawled. "Hector Bob handles only the best products and services." Even muffled by the mask, Hector Bob's voice seemed to slither up Antigone's spine. He was enjoying himself. She was not.

Antigone turned to Ryder and cocked an eyebrow.

"It'll do," he said, keeping his eye on Hector Bob.

Antigone wasted no time starting the engine.

Hector Bob ran his hand along the side of the Mustang as he slowly circled the front of the car coming to a stop next to Antigone's door. Ryder edged closer to Antigone. "This sure is some nice wheels. You know, I don't think I know anybody who's been born on Halloween before. I wore this for you, boy."

Ryder stared him in the eyeholes.

Hector Bob moved closer and casually leaned through Antigone's side to get a closer look at the dashboard of the

Mustang. More than anything in the world, Antigone wanted to hightail it out of the alley and get as far away as possible from this man who reeked of sweat and cheap cologne. But the man was crowding so close, she was bound to hit him, and she'd never run over a person with a car before. Just the thought made her squeamish. And she knew for sure that good mothers did not make a habit of running down business acquaintances, at least not in front of children.

"Yessirree, this is some wheels. This color look good on me. What say we go get a drink? Celebrate our transaction. I'll ride with you."

It was ten o'clock in the morning, a little early for local taverns to be open.

"We gotta be goin'," Ryder said.

Hector Bob tilted his head toward Ryder. Chuckling, he casually stepped back from the car, raising his hands in mock surrender. That's when Antigone realized, at some point, he'd slipped on black driving gloves. He began to reach into his coat pocket then stopped and lifted his head slightly toward the alley entrance. At the same time, Antigone heard sirens, growing ever closer. Hector Bob and Ryder exchanged another long, intense stare. "Maybe another time," Hector Bob said.

"Let's go." Ryder tapped Antigone on the shoulder. "Gun it."

Antigone pressed her foot to the accelerator, unable to shake the feeling that they might have just escaped a long walk home to Mercy. As they sped out of the alley, spitting gravel, she saw Hector Bob in the rearview mirror, waving both hands in the air, fingers shaped in peace signs.

CHAPTER 10

BANANA CREAM AMBUSH

ANTIGONE BROWN FIGURED IF she could handle Hector Bob, she could deal with Irene. Besides, Antigone had talked Nancy into coming with her. Nancy was her backup. Her backup was thirty minutes late.

So Antigone sat in the Mustang under a tree in front of Irene's house and waited. Finally, Irene opened her heavy oak front door with its black iron antique hinges and lion head knocker and yelled, "Are you stalking me?"

Antigone got out of the car and strolled up the walk. "You're not my type," she said.

"Well, come on in then." Irene pulled the door wider then turned toward the kitchen. "I've pies in the oven."

Antigone tugged the big door closed behind her. It weighed a ton. Maybe Irene just opened and closed the door as part of her fitness regimen. Irene prided herself on maintaining her size six figure. "You bake? I thought that was what Cecily was for."

"Cecily can't bake a decent pie crust to save her soul. She's strictly a cookie person."

Antigone had never been inside the Crump home. It had an echoey feeling. She stepped into the foyer and peered up into the cathedral ceiling, then looked down at the thick Oriental rug in rich colors gracing the travertine stone floor. The rug created a thick wool garden of exotic vines and flowers in luxurious reds, golds, and tans. The air was scented with a monstrous arrangement of lilies on a round table in the foyer. She passed Greek columns, holding nothing up really; they seemed to be guarding the entrance to an *Architectural Digest* living room. The living room in question was a controlled environment from the shiny baby grand in front of the big windows to the neat stacks of magazines on the coffee table. The fieldstone fireplace was large enough to roast a deer in, a thought that gave Antigone the willies.

Irene led the way past the perfect living room and into a no-less-perfect kitchen. With every step, Antigone thought of *her* house, with shoes dropped wherever someone walked out of them, cabinet doors standing open in the kitchen, window sills cluttered with her treasures—leaves, rocks, and pinecones she'd found while walking with the deer. She thought, when you took the time to really examine something, you paid it respect. And if you carried it around with you for a while, then it became a part of you. Every once in a while tidy Sam cleared off the window sills, starting the process all over again.

Three pies were sitting on the center island in Irene's big, bright kitchen—a banana cream and two lemon meringues. Irene checked a restaurant-size oven. The smell of apples and cinnamon wafted out with a gust of heat. Irene motioned Antigone toward a U-shaped banquette that seated eight easily. Like the rest of the kitchen, it was all carved wood, painted white, with flowery fabric on cushions and pillows. Antigone couldn't see the purpose in having pillows in a kitchen.

"Ice tea? Sorry, I can't offer you some pie, but we're having dinner guests tonight. Associates of Arthur's."

"No problem. I don't want the little one to develop a sweet tooth." Antigone tapped her tummy. "Sam read somewhere that whatever I eat is going straight to Junior. I mean if I eat nothing but spicy foods, the kid is likely to come out roaring fire like a dragon."

"Well, I don't know much about dragons, but I do avoid all spicy foods myself," Irene said.

"Of course, you do. You seem like a sensible woman," Antigone took a sip of tea from a Waterford crystal glass. "That's why I can't figure out what the hell is wrong with you, Irene."

Irene, sitting across the table, paused as she lifted her glass. "Pardon?"

"This book business."

Irene matched the kitchen: eggshell silk blouse and pants protected by a pristine floral bib apron with ruffles along the edge. She tugged at the bib and smoothed it. "What exactly are we talking about?"

"Just you stomping all over the Constitution with your fancy heels." Irene glanced at Antigone's scuffed hiking boots and raised an eyebrow. "I know about your little lists of banned books, Irene. I can't believe you drew Nancy into this crazy scheme of yours. And it *is* crazy. Censoring books you don't like. I don't know how you can sleep at night."

"I sleep quite well, thank you." Irene sniffed and lifted her chin. "I'm protecting the children of this town. I'm doing something worthwhile, unlike some people I know who are only interested in running low-class tourist traps and linen outlets."

"People love my tourist trap, and my sheets are eight hundred thread count."

"I'm making a difference in our community."

"You're making a mess. Do you think you'll get away with this? This is the United States of America! Americans get a tad irritable when people try to take our rights away. And we're not a quiet people. The media, the Internet, they're going to crucify Mercy."

Irene rapped the table, using one manicured fingernail like a gavel. "I would think you would understand. You're having a child. A *good* mother thinks of her children."

Antigone stiffened. "I want to protect my child *from* the world, Irene. But I also want to protect the world *for* my child."

"What a load of New Age liberal hooey."

Antigone had learned long ago to counter power with

stubbornness. You just didn't give in—when the words seem to beat you, when the teacher doesn't understand, when the kids won't leave you alone. You dig in your heels so deep it'll take a bulldozer to move you. And that's what Irene and her overdeveloped sense of entitlement would need—one of Arthur's bulldozers.

"I'm going to stop you, Irene."

"I'd like to see you try. Nobody stops me."

"Don't make this ugly. Tell Nancy to put the books back, and we'll forget this ever happened."

The two women glared at each other like boxers in the ring. The timer on the oven dinged, and both of them jumped to their feet. Irene rushed to the counter, pulled on oven mitts, and removed two apple cobblers from the oven. She placed them on the cooling racks on the granite counter by the stove then turned to Antigone. "Go back to your little deer."

Antigone knew this was a trick of the powerful: dismiss and patronize and watch your opponent slink off. She'd had a lifetime of people dismissing her. But when she came to Mercy, she had decided her slinking days were over. Her inheritance had empowered her, and now she ran a successful animal attraction and the only vegetarian restaurant within fifty miles. She and Sam also owned a textile outlet and a garage, both profitable businesses. Her eyes narrowed.

Irene smiled and leaned her hip against the counter, which featured a fancy floral motif you might find at Versailles. She crossed her arms, floppy oven mitts still on her hands.

"Think twice about taking this any further, Antigone.

You would be better off taking care of your business instead of sticking your nose in mine."

"This *is* my business."

"The world is an unpredictable place," Irene continued. "The textile mill could find another outlet for its seconds. The health inspector could take a special interest in your little restaurant. My husband could find another mechanic for his fleet."

Suddenly, Antigone felt a roaring in her head; if she had been a cartoon character, steam would have erupted from her ears. She softly rubbed her stomach to quiet herself as much as the baby. "Don't bring my family's life into this. I'm warning you, Irene."

"Or what?"

Antigone gazed around Irene's prized kitchen. There was no evidence of spilt flour on the counter or measuring cups in the sink or mixing bowls scattered about. It was spotless. Perfect. So Irene.

"You like things neat, don't you, Irene?"

Silence.

"Everything in its place."

More silence.

Antigone wrinkled her nose and dragged her hand along the cool granite countertop of the center island. "Everything tidy, contained, in control. Well, control this!" and with a sweep of her arm, she knocked a lemon meringue pie off the counter. It landed upside down on the tile floor.

Irene gasped. She straightened. Her mouth moved but no words came out.

"Oops!" Antigone looked Irene in the eye and said quietly, "I'm not going to slink off and let you and your little club ruin this town. Leave the library alone and leave my family alone, Irene." She paused, her hand dangerously close to another pie. "Back off, or things could get messy." Then Antigone started out of the kitchen.

"Antigone!" Irene screamed. "This isn't over!"

Antigone turned, and Irene smacked her in the chest with the banana cream pie. Antigone blinked. The pie slid down her body, slalomed over the bump of her pregnant belly, and plopped on the floor. The only thing that saved the second lemon meringue pie—and Irene's pristine apron—was the sure knowledge that Irene would have her up on assault charges if she dared retaliate. Bullies could dish out the pie, but they couldn't take it. So Antigone simply marched out of Irene's showcase house, dripping banana cream, leaving the heavy front door wide open.

WAITING FOR HER WHEN she drove up to the house was Nancy, parked in a rocking chair on the front porch, smoking furiously. The ashtray Antigone kept on the porch just for Nancy was overflowing with butts. Antigone climbed out of the car, and Nancy jumped to her feet.

"I'm sorry. I chickened out! You're probably mad and disappointed and," she stopped, sniffed. "Banana cream. Are you wearing banana cream?"

"Yeah." Antigone plucked the front of her sticky shirt from her chest.

Nancy's eyes rounded. "What happened?"

"This is the new fragrance from the House of Irene."

"Wow, Irene's famous for her banana cream pie, but I've never heard of her using it as a weapon before."

CHAPTER 11

REFRIGERATOR RUMBLE

RYDER HAD MADE A friend. Now how the hell had that happened? The kid's name was Ben, and he was some kind of freakin' genius. Heck, he even doodled in mathematical equations. He pretty much spooked all the teachers. Ben was everything Ryder was not: white, well off, fawned over by his mother, pushed by his father, able to glide through life without a struggle. And for some unfathomable reason, he had latched onto Ryder.

It was a late Monday afternoon in September. Ben and Ryder walked into the main office just as Mrs. Sweetings, the volunteer, was closing up shop. She threw Ryder a suspicious look then beamed at Ben. Ryder handed her Hector Bob's official documentation. She barely glanced at it. Mrs. Sweetings made a copy of the fake birth certificate, tucked it away in his file, and returned the original to Ryder. Then she said in the cheery voice she adopted for all the students, "I hope you've been having an excellent school year so far, Irwin."

Ryder replied in a mumble, "I'm here, ain't I?"

Mrs. Sweetings's smile flickered.

Outside the office, Ben grinned, "Irwin?"

"Don't go there, man," Ryder said, slinging his book bag on one shoulder and shoving open the front doors.

Ben followed. He was a short, chunky kid with wire-rim glasses. His book bag, strapped snugly on his back like a parachute, was so loaded it dragged and bumped his butt. Ben was a learning machine, and for some reason, he liked telling Ryder everything he discovered. It was like hanging with Google.

Oddly enough, Ryder realized he liked listening to Ben sometimes. He would never admit it, but he also *liked* doing homework. Man, how the mighty had fallen. In his old neighborhood, when you worked an angle, it had nothing to do with geometry.

They passed the library, one of Ryder's favorite places at Mercy High School, even if the librarian was a whack job. Libraries made him think of the Professor. The Professor would have been proud if he could see him now. The Professor believed in education. Wasn't he always telling Ryder to go to school? Wasn't he always reading books to Ryder as they sat in some cold, dirty alley? The Professor was one strange dude, but Ryder had loved him. On cold winter days, they'd taken shelter in the heated New York Public Library, like a lot of street people. But the Professor was different, and the librarians knew it. They never hassled Ryder when he was sitting at one of the long tables with the Professor. In a world where children hardly read anything more challenging than comic books and parents preferred bodice rippers to Baudelaire, the Professor with his charming smile and obvious love of books had been librarian chocolate.

Like James Bond, the Professor, even unwashed and in rags, had an unusual effect on women. It was the accent. "I could listen to him talk all day," one rich bitch do-gooder gushed as she stirred a huge pot of tomato soup in the Salvation Army kitchen. "He could read the telephone book for all I care." Such was the seduction of a British accent on American women.

The Professor could have gotten away with so much, but scams and grifts never interested him. The only thing the Professor wanted was his old cloth sack of books—his "personal collection," as he called it—and to hang out with Ryder.

There'd been so many afternoons in the library, Ryder sitting with his back against the wall so he'd have an unobstructed view of all exits, and the preoccupied Professor sitting opposite, his back exposed, a book clutched in his fingers. It was left to Ryder, thumbing through a magazine or book, to keep a casual surveillance, to watch over the Professor and his bag of books.

Now Ryder wished he'd focused less on security and more on the books in the library.

As Ryder and Ben rounded the corner of the library,

they ran smack into a pile of smelly, teen-age flesh—Art Junior and his gang. Ben, who had been rattling on about some new species of sea creature scientists had just found, immediately shut up. Ryder automatically stood straighter and stared Art Junior in the eye. He relaxed his muscles and shifted his weight forward to the balls of his feet.

"Well, well," Art Junior smirked. "Brainiac and Chicken-shit." The other boys laughed.

Ryder remained silent. He didn't move a muscle.

Art Junior edged his face closer to Ryder's. "Get somebody to haul that piece of shit car out of the ditch?"

"You didn't even hang around to see if she was hurt," Ryder snarled. "You coulda killed her."

"Who? Crazy Deer Woman? She's nuts, you know. Came right into my house and wrecked my mom's kitchen. She talks to those animals like Doctor Fucking Dolittle. And now she thinks she's going to get into it with my mom." He laughed. "I shoulda just flattened you both and done the world a favor."

"Shut the fuck up," Ryder growled.

Art Junior glanced at his friends. "Ooooh. Maybe our boy's got a thing for white meat."

Ryder started to turn away, then came spinning back around. He threw his elbow into Art Junior's nose and blood spurted. Art Junior screamed. Three of his friends stepped forward, but Art Junior, doubled over and holding his face, waved them off. Ryder dropped his book bag and lifted his fists.

Art Junior and Ryder were the same height, but that was where the similarities ended. Art Junior was a refrigerator where Ryder, after a summer of caring for the deer, was a puma—sleek, muscled, and fast. Art Junior charged with his head down. "I'm gonna kill ya, boy." But Ryder nimbly sidestepped the lump of fury and punched him in the side as he went by. Art Junior grunted and fell. Ryder waited.

Art Junior's buddies were yelling for him to get up and kick some black ass, but he just laid there. When it looked like Art Junior was finished, Ryder turned away and bent to pick up his book bag. That's when Art Junior roared to life, catching Ryder in the back and simply plowing right through, just as he'd been taught to do on the gridiron. Ryder felt Art Junior slam into him and went sprawling. Art Junior, now on top of him, started pounding, but somehow Ryder wiggled out from under the refrigerator and sprang to his feet, his fists up by his face. Art Junior slowly lumbered to his feet. Ryder was about to go for the family jewels with his foot and drop this asshole like a sack of deer feed, when the football coach came running.

"Knock it off!" He pushed his way into the middle of the group, swatting boys aside with his cap. Quickly assessing that a third of his team was involved in this mess, Coach Mac looked ready to explode. His face was nearly as red as his hair. Teachers were supposed to report all fighting for disciplinary action. "You idiots! Where are your heads at? What use you going to be to me if you get suspended for fighting?"

"He started it, Coach," Art Junior groused, wiping the blood from his face with his shirtsleeve.

Ryder didn't touch his face. He let the blood drip. Breathing hard, he simply stared at the coach.

Coach Mac eyed Art Junior with disgust. "Get to the locker room, lunkhead, and clean up. You got some laps to run. All of you. And I don't want to hear a word about this around school. Fighting on school property is automatic detention. Detention means you're out for the game that week, idiots. I'm not letting you assholes sabotage my season. Get outta here." As the football players shuffled off, the coach turned back to Ryder and pointed at him with a sausage finger. "Stay away from my boys."

Ryder merely stared at the beefy man whose belly flopped over his sweatpants and whose hair, cut military crisp, stood up like the bristles of a hairbrush, giving his freckled face an eggplant shape. "Keep 'em away from me then," Ryder replied.

The coach shook his head, slammed his cap back on, and stomped away.

Ben pulled out a white handkerchief and handed it to Ryder. Ryder looked at it for a moment then took it. He dabbed at his nose and the corner of his lip. His cheekbone felt like it was on fire, his nose was tender, and he could already feel his lip swelling. "You go get the coach?"

"I memorized the school policy handbook on my first day, especially the part about detention," Ben said.

"Of course you did."

"I figured the coach would value his team more than the rules," Ben continued. "A winning football team is a big deal in Mercy. Art Junior's an asshole, but he's an asshole who can play football."

Ryder nodded. Maybe having a genius in his corner wasn't so bad.

"You think I'll clean up good and no one'll notice?" he asked Ben.

"Not a chance."

Later, when Ryder let himself in through the kitchen door, Sam was waiting for him. "Star said there'd been some trouble. She was vague about the details."

Psychic tattle-tail. Now Sam was going to give him crap about fighting at school. But Sam just handed him a bag of frozen peas for his lip, said "Call Star. She's worried," and went back to the garage.

CHAPTER 12

THE SECRET

RYDER, BEN, AND STAR huddled on the back porch step and eavesdropped. Through the kitchen window slammed the angry voices of Sam and Antigone. Ryder had grown up in an apartment that had seen more fights than Madison Square Garden, but he had never heard one like this in the Thorne household. It made his skin crawl. His leg jiggled. He had to be ready, he told himself, the first crash of a dish hitting a wall or the smack of a hand on a cheek and he was going in. He didn't care if Sam outweighed him by forty pounds.

Antigone was determined to speak at the school board meeting the next night and call out Irene in public for banning books. Sam was against the idea.

"I don't know why you have to get involved," Sam yelled.

Antigone's voice rose with each sentence. "Because Nancy's my friend and she asked for my help. Because what Irene and her club are doing is wrong. Because I don't want my baby growing up in a world without books. And because that maniac threw a pie at me!"

"So you're going to march into the Mercy High School Auditorium and tell the whole world your deepest, darkest secret."

Ryder and Ben exchanged looks. They turned to Star, who pointedly refused to meet their eyes. "What secret?" whispered Ryder. She shrugged.

Silence. Then Sam's voice again, soft and gentle. "Haven't I kept your secret? Even though I think you could shout it from the rooftops and nobody would care."

"You're not the one who can't read," Antigone said.

What? Ryder couldn't believe it. How could that be? She owned businesses. She was smart and pretty. He knew she was educated just by the way she talked. How could this be true?

Ryder dropped his face into hands. Now a few things were beginning to make sense. The way Antigone always told him to go to Sam for help with his homework. How sometimes he saw her studying the label on a jar as if it were written in some kind of code. And how weird it was last week to walk into the kitchen and find Sam, who is not your cake-decorating kind of guy, carefully writing "Happy Birthday, Ryder" with a pastry tube on his birthday cake. Ryder had watched him for a moment then sneaked back out of the kitchen. A birthday cake was a whole new experience for

Ryder, and just the thought of it still made him feel funny inside. But the image of Chef Froot Loops was even weirder.

Sam's voice carried out the window, "It's your choice, your secret. I just don't like seeing you forced to do something you've always avoided."

"It may be the only way to convince them."

"Convince them?"

"That you can't take books away from kids," she said. "They need them."

Silence.

"Sam, this whole thing gives me that feeling inside."

"What feeling?"

"The one I used to get when I was a kid," she paused, searching for the words. "Locked out."

"Locked out?"

"Yeah, when you want something so badly and it's just on the other side of the door. The words are always on the other side of the door, Sam. And I rattle the knob and bang on the door . . ." Ryder squeezed his head harder. "When I was a kid, I was desperate to know the secrets in books. They had to be full of secrets, didn't they? Because they were so incomprehensible to me. Mysteries. I pestered my parents to read to me all the time."

"And now we're going to be parents," Sam said.

"Yeah, we are."

Ryder felt Star's hand on his knee, trying to calm his jiggling foot. He forced his foot to be still.

"What if, heaven forbid, Irene and her club are right?" Sam asked.

"What do you mean?"

"Now, hear me out, Tigg," Sam said. "As parents, we have a right to say we don't want our children exposed to smut and pornography and vulgar language. Not every book is good."

Wrong move, Sam, Ryder thought. He heard the simmer in Antigone's voice. "Do you want Irene Crump deciding which book is good enough for our child?"

"Of course not, Irene's a nut case."

"Not to mention a pie thrower."

Silence, then Sam again, an almost pleading voice.

"Don't you get it, Tigg? I don't want my child reading dirty books or watching violent television shows or listening to rap music that tells her to have sex whenever she wants."

"I want what's best for our baby, too," Antigone cried. "But wanting to preserve my child's liberty doesn't make me a bad mother."

"I never said you were a bad mother."

"Then what—." Antigone's voice changed. "This isn't about my telling people I'm dyslexic at all. You don't want me to speak against censorship—period. You *agree* with Irene."

"I didn't say that."

"You want to control what our child reads."

"Of course, I do. I don't want books filling her head with ideas that frighten me, ideas that will take her away from me." Sam's voice exploded in frustration. "Do you really want our child to read sex manuals?"

"If she has the parts, she needs to know how they work."

"Guidebooks to terrorism? Accounts of devil worship?"

"Now you're just being ridiculous."

"You're willing to throw the doors to our child's mind open to every pervert with a pen," he snapped.

"I'm protecting her by protecting her rights!"

Silence.

"You're afraid of losing her," Antigone said, finally figuring it out.

A chair was shoved aside, and Ryder leaped to his feet. "You're goddamn right, I am!" Sam shouted and then Ryder heard Sam stomping out of the room, not in their direction but toward the front door. The slam of the door shook the house.

Ryder tiptoed to the kitchen window and peeked inside. He saw Antigone bent over, hugging her pregnant belly, crying.

CHAPTER 13

A PAINE IN THE NECK

THEY WERE IN STAR'S backyard. She and her mother lived in a bungalow, two stories, small rooms, nice deck. Earthly Sims liked to barbecue and owned a gas grill that looked smart enough to cook the meat itself. When Ryder was in a mood for a charred-black hotdog, Earthly was his source.

A wooden bench ran the length of one side of the deck. It was there Star lounged, legs tucked under her chin, eyes following him as he paced up and down the yard. Ben sat on the other end of the bench, back straight, eyes unfocused.

At first, Ryder was angry that Antigone was in pain and he couldn't do anything about it. Then he began to feel something else, the calm that used to come over him when he had to face one of the Boyfriends, the men who plunged

107

through the turnstile of his mother's life. Users disguised as lovers. His mother had a weakness for beefy hotheads. When Ryder went up against them, he usually got the shit beat out of him. But that's sometimes what you had to do to protect your mother and your sister.

"Art Junior and his jerks are going to have a field day with this," he said to Ben and Star. "I can't let her do it—gettin' up there and makin' a fool of herself. We gotta stop her."

"How?" asked Star.

Ryder stopped in front of Ben. The guy was already mumbling his genius talk, and they didn't have time for that. "Is it the obligation of the liberal to guard the rights of the racist?" Ben muttered to himself.

"Ben."

"Is it the responsibility of the close-minded to protect the free thinker?"

"Ben, knock it off." Ben blinked at him through his thick glasses, a far-off look in those innocent blue eyes, so like the Professor's. Not another one, Ryder thought and felt like kicking something.

"Thomas Paine wrote . . .," Ben said.

Ryder's hand sliced the air. "I don't want to hear it."

"Paine said, 'He that would make his own liberty secure, must guard even his enemy from opposition.'" Ryder grabbed Ben by the sweatshirt and lifted him to his feet, nearly shaking him, but Ben kept talking. "'For if he violates his duty, he establishes a precedent that will reach to himself.'"

"I don't know what that shit means," Ryder shouted at him. "You're not helping."

Star jumped to her feet. She tugged on his arm. "Ryder. Ryder!"

As if just realizing where he was and what he was doing, Ryder released Ben and backed away. He raked his hands through his hair.

Ben just looked at him. "It means this is not just about books locked in a broom closet. This is about liberty and rights and all the stuff we hear people talk about when they talk about America."

"Wow," said Star.

Ryder lifted his shoulders. "I don't care about America. I don't care about books. How do we keep Antigone from speaking at that meeting?"

"I'm not sure that we can," said Ben, "short of kidnapping her."

"Then how do we help her?" asked Star.

"Are you nuts?" Ryder said. "No, we gotta keep her from embarrassing herself in front of the whole town. We gotta protect her from herself."

"But what she's doing is right," argued Star.

Ryder glared at her. "It's just books; they're not worth it."

"Antigone thinks they are," Ben said.

That's the trouble when you try to help people, Ryder thought, it gets so damn complicated.

"We need to support her. This is a noble cause," Ben said. "Besides, not every kid gets to fight censorship in his own backyard. This'll be fun."

Ryder took a deep breath to keep from throwing Ben off the deck and into Earthly's favorite butterfly bush. Earthly would kill him if he wrecked that horticultural baby. "This is not a game, man."

"Don't you see? Antigone has the right idea." Ben leaned forward. "Censorship only succeeds when it's kept in the dark. Bring it into the light. We'll pack that meeting with students and signs."

"Stand with Antigone," Star said.

Ben nodded. "Make a scene Irene Crump will never forget."

"Not to mention that cowardly, dirty-fighting son of hers," Ryder muttered.

Ben held out his fist. Ryder looked at it then gave it a bump. He glanced at Star. She was smiling at him.

CHAPTER 14

MERCY FULL

IN 1939, FEDERAL MONEY dribbled into Mercy, North Carolina, from President Franklin D. Roosevelt's Work Projects Administration and accumulated on the walls of the Mercy High School Auditorium. There it was molded into—of all things—a frieze by a then unknown artist named Remo. A little more than a foot deep, the frieze was a white plaster tapestry that encircled the auditorium about balcony level. Titled *Mercy Full,* it was a ribbon of humanity, roly-poly figures, fairly androgynous in appearance, except for the occasional necklace or apron or beard that designated gender or occupation or age. The figures were caught in various forms of work and play.

On the November evening of the school board meeting, Antigone settled back in the hard auditorium seat, gazed at the frieze circling above her, and tried to relax. She had always liked this piece of art. It told its story with pictures, shapes, and forms that she could have run her hands over if she had had a ladder tall enough and if Sam and Ryder would let her climb a ladder in her condition.

When they arrived, she'd been shocked to find the auditorium packed. She and Sam wouldn't have found seats if Nancy Sandhart hadn't been saving two beside her. She was also surprised to see a large crowd of students, which included Ryder and his friend Ben, standing in the balcony, waving signs and chanting.

Antigone leaned over and whispered to Sam, "I'm scared."

Sam squeezed her hand and tucked it in the crook of his arm. "Not too late to bail. You don't have to put yourself through this. Let's go home."

"And let all these people down? Some of them gave up their favorite television shows to be here and see me make a fool of myself."

"That's something to be proud of—beating out *America's Most Wanted*."

"After this meeting, *I'm* going to be America's Most Wanted."

Antigone had no note cards or papers. The last thing she needed to worry about was speaking *and* reading. She'd gone over what she planned to say again and again in her head. She'd given her speech a dozen times to the deer by the pond. She took several deep breaths and thought surely everyone could hear her heart beating.

"Do you think it's hot in here?" she asked Sam.

"No," he said.

Antigone patted her stomach. Let me be doing the right thing, she prayed.

IN THE BEGINNING, THE people of Mercy had thought the WPA project was a waste of taxpayers' money. In fact, upon first viewing the frieze, many were horrified and wanted the town fathers to take a jackhammer to it. Naked people in a school, they sniffed with disgust. Apparently, a scarf here and a hat there didn't cut it when it came to the sensibilities of the people of Mercy. Eventually, however, cooler heads prevailed, and through the years, the frieze became a local landmark.

When the auditorium was renovated in 1993 through a successful fund-raising drive spearheaded by the Mercy Study Club, the club hired an expert to remove fifty-four years of grime, gum, spitballs, and who knew what else the students of Mercy High had thrown, slung, and blown up there. It took the restorer five weeks, clinging to a ladder and cleaning the frieze with what looked like an electric toothbrush, to scrape away generations of juvenile high jinks.

Every time Irene Crump saw *Mercy Full,* she knew the restorer had been worth every penny. Some of the club members had complained about flying in a frieze expert from New York; surely, they said, there were local people who could do the same thing with a sponge, a hose, and a bucket of Spic and Span. But Irene had insisted that the job be done right. "This is a work of art, for goodness sake," she told her husband Arthur, "an artistic interpretation of our town."

In fact, art historians considered *Mercy Full* to be one of the finest pieces of public art to come out of the WPA. As one scholar noted, "It glorifies the everyman in all his small town splendor. It's Norman Rockwell meets the Pillsbury Dough Boy."

Irene admitted that the restorer had been a strange fellow to deal with, always wearing a headlamp strapped to his bald head, even while he ate lunch at the O. Henry Café. His glasses had been as thick as his New York accent. When you looked into his eyes, it was like staring into fish eyes through the magnification of water and glass—startling and other-worldly. But he knew his way around plaster, friezes, and art. He pronounced Mercy's pride and joy "some piece of work."

Irene had always felt close to Mercy's only piece of public art. She couldn't explain it and long ago had stopped trying to get Arthur to understand how special *Mercy Full* was to her. She only knew that when she looked at the frieze, during every school function, she felt something stir inside her. It made her feel a part of something bigger. The figures in the tableau were creating a new world, a place where families were wholesome and towns were alive with commerce, education, spiritual growth, and civic pride. The frieze stretched before Irene like a dream of what the real Mercy could be. Except in the real Mercy, everyone was wearing clothes. Thank goodness.

That's what this meeting was really about, Irene told the Study Club, which was heavily represented in the first two rows. "This meeting is about taking back our community, our children, our very lives. It's about saying no to sexual perversion, crime, drugs, welfare mothers, juvenile delinquency, disrespect, cults, abortion—all the obscenities we've allowed to steal into our lives through the back door of the Bill of Rights."

RYDER DIDN'T KNOW WHY, but he liked the chubby art people marching around on the auditorium walls. Ben had told him that in Mercy—you either loved the frieze or hated it. As Ryder listened to a reporter who identified himself as Dash Morgan interview Ben, he also kept an eye on Antigone. She leaned over and said something to the librarian, Nancy Sandhart. Sandhart shook her head. He could have told Antigone she wasn't getting any help from that corner. In his old neighborhood, Sandhart would be considered a liability—someone who wouldn't come through for you in the end and, in fact, would probably get your ass shot off.

He turned his attention back to Ben and the reporter. Ben had organized the protest and was considered the spokesperson. There were about thirty students gathered in the balcony. Ryder didn't know many of them. But, he had to admit, they were an excited bunch. They carried signs: "Free Our Books," "Our Town Shows No Mercy to Books," "Is This Russia?" They chanted, "No more censorship! No more censorship!" Ryder noted that Art Junior and his clowns weren't among the protesters.

"We're here because this is our school, Mr. Morgan,"

Ryder heard Ben say, "and we're not going to tolerate people banning books."

A girl beside Ryder, dressed like a French Resistance freedom fighter—beret pulled over her short, spiky hair; long, black wool coat with a scarf dangling to her knees; and gloves with the fingertips cut out—chimed in, "Yeah, you can't tell us to be good little citizens in social studies class and then pull fascist moves in the library."

"How do you know books have been removed from the library?" Morgan asked.

"We have our sources," Ben said.

A boy in a flannel shirt lifted a pierced eyebrow and said, "Yeah, man, book banning is, like, so uncool."

Ben smiled at Dash Morgan and shrugged. "Our parents have screwed up—just about everything. Global warming, AIDS, corruption in governments, racism, genocide, ethnic cleansing, financial meltdown. How are we going to solve these problems? We need more information, not less. More books, not fewer."

The reporter jotted something down in the little notebook he carried. "It's a light year leap from a few missing books to genocide."

"Genocide's all about exterminating those who are different," Ben retorted. "Censorship exterminates ideas that are different. Being different is something teenagers know about."

"We were born different," Resistance Girl piped up.

"Somebody has to stop the ruin, man," nodded Flannel Boy.

"Mr. Morgan," Ben swept his arm to encompass the walls and the chubby people of the Mercy frieze, "FDR, the guy who gave us this, said once in a speech, 'Books may be burned and cities sacked, but truth, like the yearning for freedom, lives in the hearts of humble men and women. No people in all the world can be kept eternally ignorant or eternally enslaved.'"

"Yeah," said Flannel Boy, "fuck that slavery shit."

Ryder rolled his eyes.

❧

"I HATE MEETINGS," NANCY mumbled, rummaging in her purse for a cigarette. Antigone watched her friend, now clutching a pack of cigarettes, eye the exit. "This job is making me crazy."

"Duck into the girls' room. I'll save your seat," Antigone said.

Nancy made a face. "You know what that's like."

Nancy claimed the girls' rest room smelled of high school girls, sanitary napkins, and semen. At least that's what she imagined ever since she discovered a used condom in the corner of one of the stalls. Nancy had always had her doubts about the efficacy of the janitorial staff. Now, she said, she went to the bathroom twice before leaving home in the mornings, with the idea of delaying the inevitable for as long as possible.

"I hate books," Antigone mumbled as Irene Crump, the chair of the school board, called the meeting to order at precisely seven o'clock. Antigone had spent her whole life avoiding public appearances. She *really* did not want to be here. She *really* did not want to do this. Reading was her nemesis, wasn't it? Antigone could hear her mother's voice in her head: "A smart woman always carries a book and a credit card—the book for when she has nothing to do and the card for when she has too much to do. Oh, and darling, she always wears moisturizer."

Antigone fingered the round stone in her left pocket, lifted it to her cheek, closed her eyes, and enjoyed its cool smooth surface. At least, she thought, I moisturized this morning.

All day Antigone had been thinking of her parents. She had tried to call her mother but never got through. She left a message. She didn't know exactly what she wanted to tell them: "Hey, Mother, I'm going to share my biggest secret today. Can you believe I'm doing this for some books?"

As Antigone mulled over her love/hate relationship with the written word, Irene cruised through the agenda. When she came to the call for new business, Antigone imagined the packed auditorium grew quieter. She feared stages and the front of classrooms. She hated microphones. Still, she made her way to the microphone placed in the center aisle facing the school board up on the stage. In her hand was the green marbled stone with white veins that she'd found one day by the pond. She imagined the forces of nature caressing this simple stone as she was doing. Her heart was galloping, and her breath was coming in small shaking whispers. She poured her fears and stresses into that rock, hoping to steel her resolve.

To further combat her stage fright, Antigone looked at each board member and imagined that he or she was a deer.

She pretended she was at the pond, and they were simply listening and grazing. The school board was like a herd. There was the old buck, Howard, a hardware store owner, who thought all of their problems could be solved by taking a chainsaw to every television in town. Then there were the young bucks: Gary, the only dentist in town and president of the Chamber of Commerce; Hank, an accountant; and Luther, a foreman at the mill. They jostled for power, glory, and attention. They couldn't wait for Howard to go down in the next election. They had children in kindergarten, in middle school, and on the high school soccer team. The males could be counted on to agree on one thing: money. The teachers got too much of it, the administration didn't know what to do with it, and the taxpayers providing it ought to have something to say in how it was spent.

The females on the board—Ellen, a homemaker/volunteer; Kalinda, an artist; and Irene Crump—were all mothers. In the bucks' opinion, mothers were entirely too soft, too willing to defend children, and too quick to demand action. The problem with does, the bucks thought, was that they were always putting children first and that's no way to run a school.

Antigone cleared her throat, clutched her stone, and began to speak. The microphone amplified her words into the auditorium, and, suddenly, the room caught its breath.

"I have a complaint," Antigone paused, took a shaky breath, and proceeded. "Irene and the Mercy Study Club have pressured librarian Nancy Sandhart into removing certain books from the school library."

There was a rustling in the crowd.

"They're removing books *they* don't like. Banning books. Like the Nazis did."

A few parents gasped. Heads swiveled toward the school board. Irene tugged on the hem of her jacket. "There are no Nazis in the Mercy Study Club. We are making an effort to protect our children from inappropriate literature. Smut."

"Smut? These books are *dirty* books?" a woman in the audience asked.

"If they're dirty, what are they doing in the library in the first place?" a man growled.

Antigone forced herself to breathe calmly. Her insides were so wired she believed she could hear her baby's heartbeat. "These are good old American books. Classics. Award winners." She recited a list of the books, which Nancy had helped her memorize. "*1984. The Catcher in the Rye. Of Mice and Men. To Kill a Mockingbird.*"

"Winning a prize doesn't make it good literature," Irene retorted.

Someone shouted from the audience. "This is America. We don't ban books!"

The students erupted with shouts of "Yeah," and "You said it, man," and "Nazi bitch." They began chanting again. "No more censorship! No more censorship!" Some of the parents joined in. Antigone turned to look up at Ryder, who was watching her in silence from the balcony. She gave him a nervous smile. He did not smile back.

Irene began hammering on the table with her gavel. "That's enough. Quiet!" Coach Mac and the vo-tech instructor approached the students and motioned for them to settle down. Antigone glanced at Dash Morgan, who was scribbling furiously in his notebook, then at the book club members, who had begun to look uncomfortable. The burst of support washed through her. She relaxed her grip on the stone in her hand.

When the room had quieted, Hank the accountant faced Antigone. "Antigone, this really isn't the place for this discussion. We have a review committee whose job is to decide what books our school will or will not carry."

"Irene's group didn't go through a review committee."

"Well, we'll rectify that right now," Hank said with a frown to Irene. "Both the list of books you've just recited *and* any challenges presented by Irene's group will be forwarded to the committee members, and they can make the decision."

"Hank," Antigone said, "that sounds like a political dodge to me."

"Yeah," said a large woman taking up two seats at the end of the third row. "I'd like to know where this board stands on smut."

The chairs on the stage began to creak under the weight of seven shifting bottoms.

"Of course, we're against smut," said Howard in exasperation.

Gary the dentist agreed. "Yes, none of us want our children reading pornography. I'm sure Antigone doesn't want that either."

Ellen, wearing a patient Earth Mother expression on her face, leaned forward. "Antigone, you're having a baby soon. Surely, you want to protect it."

Antigone cast a glance at Sam. "That's why I'm here. I-I-don't think these books are indecent. Books are simply the keepers of someone's ideas, and, even if we don't agree with those ideas, we have to protect their right to express them. Even if I hated the ideas in those books, I'd still fight for their right to exist."

Irene said in exasperation. "Have you read some of this trash?"

Antigone lifted her shoulders. "Probably not."

"Then I suggest you do a little research before you pass judgment," Irene retorted

Antigone's hand tightened on the stone. She looked down, took a deep breath, then lifted her head. "I would, Irene, but you see, I can't read." It was as if someone had sucked the air from the room. Irene's mouth dropped open, then quickly snapped shut. "I'm dyslexic. I may not know everything about the books on the banned list, but I know about censorship. I've lived with it all my life. Words on the page move when I try to read them. Sometimes I can get the dancing words to behave, and sometimes they defeat me. I depend a lot on Sam."

She looked at her husband. "I've always been at the mercy of others to help me because I can't easily access all the different opinions and pieces of information out there. I don't want my child to be limited—whether by a disability or by someone else's idea of what makes good literature."

Antigone looked from the school board to the people crammed into the auditorium. "You don't realize what gifts books are. They set you free. Doesn't it mean anything that even though I sometimes hate books—and believe me, they've caused a lot of misery in my life—I'm still standing here defending them?"

Irene stammered for a moment then recovered. "We have the right to decide what our children will read."

"What *your* child will read, Irene, but not mine," Antigone said.

Antigone could hear the whispers growing all around her.

She can't read? I never knew.

But she runs all those businesses . . .

She doesn't have children yet; she doesn't know what she's talking about.

My Johnny has a reading disability. It's nothing to be ashamed of.

Antigone closed her eyes, trying to shut out the remarks seeming to grow louder and crowding in on her. When she opened them, Sam was pushing his way to her side. In the balcony, she saw Ryder stir, making his way toward the exit.

Irene banged the gavel again.

Kalinda the artist said, "I think Antigone's right. We can't go around banning books."

The students began chanting again and thrusting fists in the air: "Keep America cool, keep America cool, keep America cool!"

"Order! Order!" Irene shouted. The crowd wasn't listening. The whispers grew into arguments all over the auditorium.

We're not Nazis, for gawdsakes.

Then stop acting like one.

Hey, I'm Jewish.

Then you ought to know better.

Better than what? Lighten up, lady. We're talking about a few dirty books.

Who says they're dirty?

Who decides what's indecent anyway?

We do. It's our community.

This isn't supposed to happen in America. We don't do censorship.

It happens more than you think.

Wait until the press gets a hold of this.

Gary, the chamber president, cast an anxious glance in Dash Morgan's direction. "Now, we don't want to get a reputation for being close-minded. Book banning is bad for the community's image."

Irene raised her chin in disdain. "I'd rather be a little close-minded and keep our children's minds from rotting with disgusting ideas than worry about our image, Gary. This is *our* town. We decide what we will or will not tolerate."

"No, Irene," Antigone said, "the Constitution decides. I have to tolerate your ideas—even though they're wrong—and you have to tolerate mine. Because we live in a democracy."

Irene exploded, "Don't go waving a flag in my face, Antigone Brown, you and your strange animals and vegetarian food!"

"I've known you to order tofu take-out," Antigone said.

The crowd laughed.

Irene gasped, "That's for Arthur."

Hank placed his hand over the microphone in front of Irene, but Antigone could still hear him. "For crissakes,

Irene, what have you gotten us into? Throw the issue to the review committee and be done with it."

He turned to the auditorium and said with a placating smile, "We'll turn this matter over to the review committee. In the meantime, I move for adjournment. It's bedtime."

TWO HOURS AFTER THE crowd shuffled out of the auditorium, Nancy Sandhart woke with stabbing pains in her chest.

She clawed at Bob snoring beside her. "My heart! My heart!"

Her husband peered at her through one eye and said, "What?"

"Hospital! Hospital! Now."

He flung the blanket aside, fell out of bed, and snatched up jeans, a shirt, and the car keys. Helping Nancy into a robe and slippers, the barefooted Bob then carried his wife to the car. The Sandharts lived in the country on a farm where Bob grew up. The hospital in Mercy was fifteen miles away. He figured he could make better time than the EMTs. He ignored stop signs and hit an opossum. He didn't stop. As he tore through the dark night at eighty miles per hour on crazy narrow county roads, his wife slumped in the passenger seat, clasping her chest and praying, "I don't want to die. I don't want to die."

After running a battery of tests, the doctor put Nancy on oxygen and gave her a shot to calm her. The young Pakistani doctor, pulling his second twelve-hour shift in emergency, diagnosed that Nancy's heart was not turning against her. She had had an anxiety attack.

"But it felt so terrible," Nancy trembled.

"Are you sure?" asked Bob uneasily. "Maybe we need a second opinion."

The doctor gave them a weary, boyish grin. "I assure you, Mr. Sandhart, I'm not worried about your wife. I know this is a scary feeling. But all the tests check out normal. She needs some peace and quiet. No worries. Does she have a stressful job?"

"Incredibly stressful," Nancy said.

"Well, it's not brain surgery," Bob growled.

The doctor glanced at the chart. "Let's keep you overnight, Mrs. Sandhart. Just to be safe. Once again, this is nothing to worry about. It's just a sign to take it easy. Do something soothing. Be kind to yourself. Take a bubble bath. Read a book."

"Don't talk to me about books," Nancy moaned.

Two days later Nancy Sandhart, who had been an employee of the Mercy school system for ten years, gave in to her husband's nagging and resigned from her position as librarian of the Mercy High School Media Center.

Now, she told herself, she could smoke all day if she wanted. She wondered why that didn't make her happier.

CHAPTER 15

THE DAY THE WORDS WOULDN'T STOP

RYDER WAS MAD. HE'D grabbed a hammer from Sam's tool bench, and now, standing by the junked shell of a Honda Accord in the field behind the garage, he was swinging. His breathing became fast and sweat popped out on his forehead and still he pounded. With each dent, he swung harder. His arms began to ache, and still he swung.

"What the hell are you doing?" Sam roared over the noise, approaching through the tract of weeds, metal sculptures, and half-destroyed cars.

Ryder kept hammering.

"Ryder!"

"I hate this," Ryder yelled back.

"What?"

"This shit with Antigone," Ryder whacked the hood. "I can't freaking believe it. Why didn't her parents *do* something? Why didn't they help her?" Ryder stopped to catch his breath. His arms trembled. He took a step back and bumped into one of Sam's pieces of junk art. He didn't know what it was supposed to be—letters whirling to the sky like some exploding alphabet soup.

Sam shoved his hands in his pockets. "They tried. Some cases of dyslexia are worse than others. Antigone's is pretty bad." Sam shrugged and stared at him. "She's got her tricks to survive."

Ryder knew about survival and the tricks you played on yourself and others.

"Yeah? Like what?"

Sam told him some of Antigone's tricks: learning the alphabet by shaping the letters in clay, listening to audio books, using tape recorders, taking oral school exams. "Actually, she can read; it just takes concentration and time. The letters are always jumping around on the page."

"We should never have let her get up in front of those people," Ryder said.

"It was her decision."

For some reason, Ryder imagined he saw the Professor's face in the reflection of the dented hood. He stepped forward and began pounding again. "I told him: look out for numero uno. She's got no more sense. I was always pullin' him out of shit, too."

"Who?" Sam asked.

Ryder ignored him.

From the moment they met in a New York movie house on a cold January day, Ryder had looked out for the old man known only on the street as the Professor. Ryder had been there to get warm; the Professor had been there for the show. The Marx Brothers. They'd both slipped in through a back door with a faulty latch. It was a day that changed Ryder's life. He made his first friend during that twenty-four-hour festival of eyebrow wagging, horn honking, and cigar wiggling that held Ryder spellbound. He liked the way Groucho and his brothers were always pulling something over on somebody. They swam in silliness—a pool that didn't exist in Ryder's harsh world.

Ryder always thought the Professor would have been good in a Marx Brothers movie. He was the perfect mark—born unsuspecting. No, that's not right. The Professor knew shit happened, but he *chose* not to see it. He lived in the here and now, dragging around that sorry sack of books wherever he went, embracing each moment as if he were experiencing it for the first time.

Pushing thoughts of the Professor aside, Ryder stopped hammering. "I don't understand her," he said.

"Don't worry about it. I'll look after Antigone," Sam said, digging through his pockets and offering a handful of Froot Loops to Ryder.

The boy hesitated, threw the hammer on the hood, then scooped up the cereal. "Well, you're doing a piss poor job of it."

"Ain't that the truth," Sam said. They stood, munching cereal and staring out at the rusting sculptures.

EACH DAY THE ROUTINE that was Ryder's life became more a part of him. Once, the unexpected was the norm—a drugged-out mother's slap, a push by a cop when he didn't get the answer he wanted, somebody on the street harassing him about one bullshit thing after another. Now, the unforeseen took him by surprise. This was not good, Ryder knew. Complacency (last week's vocabulary word) made a man weak and vulnerable. It made him worry about a woman who couldn't even read yet stood up for a bunch of stupid books. He knew the dangers of relaxing, of getting comfortable, of becoming involved, and yet he continued on—going to school; hanging out with Star and Ben; taking care of the deer; looking after Antigone. She was seven months pregnant, and Sam and Ryder refused to let her lift anything heavier than a toothbrush.

That was why he had begun to hate the books kids were bringing to Antigone. Kids, sitting around the dinner table, listening to their parents talk about the school board meeting and the banned books, were scared. They were afraid that their own book collections were next on the Study Club's list. So, they had begun dropping off books, even some from their parents' bookshelves. The books were everywhere at the O. Henry Café and Deer Farm, in Antigone's house, in Star's room. Star called the stacks of books growing higher each day, Antigone's Bookhenge. "Like Stonehenge," she told him. "Only made of books. Stonehenge, that's in England, is probably full of all kinds of cool vibes. Stonehenge is a mystery."

Ryder wasn't a fan of mystery. In fact, it bugged the hell out of him. The other day as he was stepping out the front door, he nearly tripped over a kid, stooped, carefully setting a book on the porch. He was the most miserable excuse for a kid that Ryder had ever seen: not a muscle in his body, freakish red hair that stood out in every direction, thick glasses held together at one corner with duct tape.

"What do you want?" Ryder snapped.

"Um, I'm Stanley," the kid said.

"So?"

"I want you to keep my book with your books. Star's in my class, and she said it was okay."

"She did, huh?"

Stanley held out his book. It was as sorry looking as the kid. Its pages were three-hole punched and tied together with dental floss. The cardboard cover was made from a cereal box. The front was decorated with crayoned moons and stars; "Too Many Words by Stanley" was printed in lousy handwriting. Ryder didn't want to touch it.

Still, Stanley shoved it at him, and before he could say, "no way," the kid was gone. Stanley was faster than he looked.

Ryder marched over to Star's house and picked up a stone to toss at her window. He and Star never knocked on doors. Before he could wind up, she flung open the window, leaned out, and smiled. "Hey."

"Don't hey me," Ryder said. "Get down here. Some

squirrelly kid left this, and I sure as hell don't want it." He flung the book on the ground.

A few moments later, Star came running out of the house. She picked up the book and stared at the cover. "Stanley?"

"Skinny, carrot top."

"That's Stanley."

"I'd appreciate it if you didn't tell the whole world they could dump their shit at Antigone's. She's got enough crap to deal with."

Star grinned. "You're such a grouch. Come on." She led him inside and up to her room. They sat down on the floor, under the window, their backs against the wall. All around them in Star's room were stacks of books. Bookhenge. "Stanley's a worrier. He's afraid his mom will take his books away."

"Fool. Like who'd want this?"

"Stanley's a good writer," she said. "Read it to me."

"I ain't readin' this. I don't *do* out loud."

"Please, Ryder," she said, her hand settling on his arm. She probably didn't realize that she held him chained to her with the lightest touch. In that moment, he flashed to an alley on a cold night, to the Professor and his powerful voice building a fire of words to keep them warm through the night. That night the words had come from James Fenimore Cooper telling the story of Indians and honor. The Professor had loved that book.

"Get comfortable," Ryder said gruffly. Star didn't hesitate to wiggle into a cozy position. He watched her close her eyes. He began, his voice winding out of the canyons of Bookhenge.

One day I woke up, and there were too many words. Words tumbled out of my mouth, and I couldn't stop them. I hurled words all day long. My mom said, "Stanley, we can't have this. There are words all over the carpet."

"I can't help it," I cried. I spewed words all over my mom. She screamed and ran to change her clothes. She took me to the doctor. The doctor examined me. He performed all kinds of tests. He said he'd never seen anything like it. I was a medical mystery.

The doctor wanted to give me a pill to stop the words. He wasn't happy with me. The words had filled up the waiting room, and the other mothers were complaining. He said there may be one side effect from the pill: It may stop the words completely. Like never talk again. Like wordless forever.

I said I didn't want the pill. But my mom said, "It's for the best."

"Why?" I said. "What's wrong with words?"

My mom and the doctor said too many words are dangerous. Uncontrollable is not good, they said. "What if everyone just said whatever popped into their heads?" my mom said. "It could get messy."

I refused to take the pill. And because I am taller than both my mom and the doctor, they couldn't make me. My mom said, "We'll see what your father has to say about this," and took me home.

By the time my dad got home, the house was full of words. They were spilling out of the windows. They had flattened the door. My mom said, "I can't breathe around all these words." My dad was not too happy either. People had been throwing words at him all day at work. He was tired of it. He said, "That's it, young man," and tossed me a sleeping bag. He sent me to the backyard.

And still the words came.

The neighbors called the police. The police said, "Sorry." They didn't want to fill up their jail with words. "It wouldn't be good for the other prisoners," the officers said.

On the second day, the talk show hosts and news anchors came. They wanted to interview me. "No," I said, sitting on my sleeping bag in the backyard. So instead they interviewed my mom and my dad. And my doctor. And my first grade teacher. And some expert on vocabulary diseases.

On the third day, the religious people came. They called me a prophet. "Come be on our evangelical show," they said.

"Why?" I said. "I'm just a regular boy."

On the fourth day, everyone left me alone. I was tired and hungry. I couldn't eat because the words wouldn't stop. My voice was nearly gone. I sat on my sleeping bag and began to cry. The words used my sobs like sleds, and I wanted to die.

By the seventh day, I began to feel light-headed. I listened to the birds. I think my words were flying with them. My words rose into the trees and sat in the branches. They floated to the sky. And I began to feel light of heart, too. The words slowed. They hugged me. They made a shield around me. I was no longer tired or hungry or unhappy.

At last, I knew. The words were not the disease. They were the cure.

RYDER CLOSED THE BOOK. Star was silent. "Well," Ryder said, "it ain't *The Last of the Mohicans.*"

CHAPTER 16

I READ BANNED BOOKS

MORE AND MORE OFTEN these days, Irene Crump woke up tired. Dragging herself from the king-size bed, she went over the day's schedule in her mind. Alice, her seven-year-old daughter, had soccer practice then dance lessons. Heaven knew what Art Junior was up to today in that black behemoth with the roaring motor and the roll bar that reminded his mother, by its very existence, how fragile life is and how invincible young drivers believe themselves to be.

In addition, she had to take a shift at the library. The Study Club members were filling in as temporary librarians until a replacement could be found for Nancy Sandhart. Irene couldn't believe that woman had resigned and left them with this mess. She heard Cecily, the maid, arrive as Arthur left for the golf course. Although it was November, there was plenty of golf to be squeezed out of the year yet. On a good day, Arthur could play nine holes before his pager started beeping with news of calamity on the construction site. He played golf like he built houses: hell-bent. He drove a golf cart like a backhoe, causing other golfers to leap out of his path. Some days, she just couldn't deal with Arthur's *energy,* oddly enough, the very exuberance that had attracted her in the first place. Arthur spent all day surrounded by "idiots" (one of his kinder terms) who delivered the wrong doors, accidentally chopped through power lines, and nailed their shirtsleeves to the siding—and with each challenge he seemed to grow stronger.

Irene stretched, shoved her arms into a thick terry robe, and trudged into her dressing room. She couldn't shake the feeling of foreboding she'd had since last night's dinner with Arthur's new business associate and his wife. Irene remembered the wife's covetous expression as she studied the Italian tiles in the solarium. The husband couldn't take his eyes off the teak paneling in the library. "There's something about all that wood," he had said. "Makes you feel manly." She knew the signs—the couple would make an offer on the house, in a week, a month, six months, but an offer *was* coming.

Irene and Arthur had never officially put any of their unique homes on the market. People just saw them and wanted them. In the paint-by-numbers world of tract housing, an Arthur Crump house was a Gauguin. A lush architectural masterpiece where the floor plans were exciting, the cathedral ceilings soared, and the baths outnumbered the occupants.

And when Irene complained that they had just moved three years ago, Arthur would pat her bottom and say, "Christ, Irene, they're offering triple what it cost us. I'll build you another house."

Arthur Crump loved to build houses for his wife—and to sell them out from under her.

Irene grimaced and tugged on the belt of her bathrobe. In twenty years of marriage, she had maintained a respectable figure, had always voted the same as her husband, and had decorated eight homes. Unlike the early days, she wasn't involved in the business anymore, except for fiddling with paint chips and selecting tile for Arthur's next masterpiece. She studied her reflection in the bathroom mirror. Where had that other woman gone, the one who worked in a crowded trailer on the construction site, who verbally skinned lazy subcontractors without giving it a second thought, who worked with joy keeping accounts and picking up lumber scraps on Saturday mornings? In those early days, all their energy—and money—went into the next house. She and Arthur often had gone without to make payroll for the crew. Her privileged background had not prepared her for that kind of life—so she had no inkling how it would make her feel to build something with her own hands, to sacrifice next to another for the sake of something bigger than you both.

Suddenly, Irene had the desire for a bologna sandwich on white bread and a beer. That was often dinner in those days, a meal she and Arthur shared, just the two of them, sitting on the floor in the middle of a house, barely framed. If she closed her eyes, she could hear the crickets coming out for the evening, their calls replacing the ringing of hammers. She could smell the fatty luncheon meat and taste the sharp beer. She could hear Arthur telling her his dreams. She could . . .

Irene walked into the shower—a small pink marble rotunda with a domed ceiling—and adjusted the water temperature. Water blasted from six gold showerheads mounted on the curved walls. She sank down on an ergonomic shower bench curved perfectly to fit the human spine, leaned her head against the wall, and closed her eyes. She often said her morning prayers in this position. "Please, Lord, make sure Cecily doesn't screw up the puff pastry for dinner tonight, and let this be a quiet day in the library without all those gum-chewing, smart-aleck kids. Finally, Lord don't let that couple from last night take my house." She thought of her precious solarium. "Why does everything have to change, God, just when I get things the way I like them?"

It was while Irene was toweling off that God dropped an idea on her. Sometimes Irene got these feelings, so strong that it seemed someone was talking to her. No voices. She wasn't one of *those* crackpots. She could only describe it as guidance, and it usually came when she was feeling low, frustrated, or ready to scream. And she had discovered, through the years, that when she followed this intuition, she almost always felt better, saner, happier.

Today, she knew she needed to stop by the bookstore, The Last Page. Arthur didn't like her to shop there. "Stick to the Book-of-the-Month, mail-order; it'll keep you out of trouble," he said.

"But I don't want all those nasty books about courtroom

drama, drug dealers, and dinosaurs eating tourists," Irene complained. She liked books in which men and women loved each other to the end of time and then some; where a husband didn't sell a wife's home and sanctuary. Besides, mail-order didn't provide the pick-me-up she found in the bookstore. She went to the bookstore to feel some control over her life.

Still recoiling from the avaricious light in the eyes of last night's guests, Irene swallowed one of her antidepressants and told herself she deserved a little boost.

WHEN IRENE ARRIVED AT The Last Page, she couldn't believe her eyes. She elbowed in between two women who were gaping at the window display. Irene spotted Cassandra, the bookstore owner, through the window. Noticing Irene standing on the sidewalk, Cassandra smiled, waved at her, and pointed to the red button pinned to her chest, which proclaimed "I read banned books."

Irene frowned. She focused on the display. The entire window replicated a garbage dump with a banner stretched across the top: "Censorship: It's a Terrible Waste." The women standing beside Irene wrinkled their noses in distaste. Books, wrapped in plain brown wrappers, mingled among old wine bottles, crushed beer cans, soiled paper napkins, and other refuse.

On each brown wrapper was written the name of a book that had been banned and the year it had been challenged. *The Sun Also Rises*, 1930, 1933 (burned in Nazi bonfires), 1953, 1960.

Again with the Nazis. Irene wanted to scream.

The Bible, 1624, 1926, 1952, 1953, 1978, 1986, 1992.

"I don't believe it, Evelyn," one of the women beside her exclaimed. "*The Bible!*"

"There's a lot of fooling around in the Old Testament," Evelyn said.

Hansel and Gretel, 1992 ("teaches children to kill witches and paints witches as child-eating monsters").

"Well, I always did think those Grimm fairy tales were— grim. They frighten even me," said Evelyn's friend. "I won't allow my son to read them to my granddaughter when he visits my house. Of course, he reads them to her when they get home. And then he wonders why she has nightmares. I've always said stick with Mother Goose. I mean, nobody was ever killed with a hot cross bun."

Evelyn frowned. "I'm sure these days they can even find something wrong with sweet old Mother Goose. Take that 'Old Woman in a Shoe.' With all those kids crammed in there, if that's not a case for child abuse, I don't know what is."

Irene listened to the two women and pondered what could be done about this disgusting display. Arthur would tell her it was free enterprise and to cool her jets. Irene felt the heat rising in her. This was just plain wrong. She and her club were knocking themselves out to maintain a modicum of decency in Mercy. Didn't people realize that the civilized world was teetering on an abyss, and it was just this kind of thinking that could tip it into chaos?

The bell over the door was still jingling when Irene marched up to Cassandra, "What is the meaning of that?" She pointed to the window.

Cassandra finished with a customer and turned. "Don't you love the display, Irene? I was at the school board meeting. My daughter's in the same grade as Art Junior, you know. Listening to all those people made me think that we really need an open discussion on censorship."

"Open discussion?" Irene snarled.

"I don't think my customers know how important this issue is. People put their heads in the sand. Of course, no one believed the Nazis burned books either—at first."

Irene gasped. "Are you comparing the concerned citizens of Mercy with Nazis?"

"Of course not, Irene. That's just crazy talk."

"You know what's *not* crazy? Wanting to protect our children."

Irene was so disturbed by the conversation and the window display that she spun around and stomped from the store. In her car, she sat, gripping the steering wheel. Finally, she took a few deep breaths and opened her purse for the car keys. That's when she saw the repent cards. She'd forgotten the whole reason she had come to The Last Page. She pulled out the cards and fanned them in her hand. She'd brought enough to place two cards in each book in the New Age section or, as she called it, the devil's bookshelf. Normally, she stuck only one card in each book. But today, she had planned to plant one sticking out of the top of the books in plain view as a decoy for Cassandra to find and a second tucked between the pages, a booby trap ready to spring on unsuspecting sinners, a bomb of God's truth waiting to explode and shower the debris of righteousness on its victims.

Then she'd seen that horrid window. And now, here she was, sitting in the Mercedes with her unused repent cards, feeling even worse than when she started out. And this trip was supposed to make her feel better.

Something inside Irene snapped. She was not without resources. She would go home and start the Study Club's phone tree immediately. When Cassandra lost all of the Study Club members' business, she might not be so smug.

CHAPTER 17

TOFU THANKSGIVING

O N Thanksgiving Day, Antigone was up to her elbows in relatives. Jonas and Marian Thorne, Sam's parents, had driven up from Florida in their white van packed with coolers of "regular" food, as the carnivorous Thornes put it. Antigone's parents, Annaliese and Henry Brown, had flown in from Massachusetts to the airport in Charlotte and rented a hybrid car. They brought a worn leather satchel (her father's) and a new rolling briefcase (her mother's) packed with books, academic journals, and student papers to read. This was the equivalent of two storm fronts converging on Antigone's dinner table.

The deer nudged Antigone's bulging coat pockets, searching for more of the small red apples she and Ryder had brought back from a trip into the North Carolina mountains. The trip to Annie's Produce Stand was an autumn ritual, roller coasting over narrow roads to buy five bushels of apples and a half dozen jugs of apple cider. Annie, of weathered face and quick smiles, always asked about William and always sent Antigone home with an extra bag of squash. "Tell William I'll see him next week," Annie said with a wink. "I'll deliver those other bushels he ordered personally."

In the fall, the menu at the O. Henry Café overflowed with apple pies, baked apples, apple bran muffins, apple pancakes, applesauce, onion apple soup. William tried any recipe that called for apples and included apples in many that didn't.

Apples were also a favorite treat of the deer. While William cooked Thanksgiving dinner, Henry and Annaliese Brown laughed as the young ones bumped against their daughter. "All right," she said, pulling out two apples. The apples were balanced on the flat of her palms for only a second before they were snatched away. Of course, the fawns' daring emboldened the others, which had been hanging back because of the unfamiliar scent of Antigone's parents. Soon, all three of them were surrounded by apple-crazy, core-crunching deer.

Antigone contemplated her parents with a smile. Although the traditional Thanksgiving Day dinner at her house was noted on the Thornes' calendar, probably years in advance, her parents played it loose when it came to holidays. Some holidays they had blown off entirely, phoning at the last minute, making excuses in preoccupied voices that Antigone recognized from years of benign inattention. This year, however, it was different. They were going to be grandparents, and their only child was having her first child. The ardent researchers and popular lecturers suddenly, and unexpectedly, found themselves obsessed with things requiring cuddling and cooing.

The deer crowded closer, sniffing Henry's tweed jacket and licking Annaliese's black designer pants. Neither seemed to notice. Antigone came from people who seldom concerned themselves with domestic details. Henry ignored the state of his clothes, and Annaliese never understood why she should be concerned about laundry when there were maids and dry cleaners.

Henry Brown, grandson of an affluent New England merchant, was sturdy and straight. His hands were small for a man and quick, the better to work a calculator. His eyes were kind, if somewhat distracted, behind round tortoise shell glasses. They were an unusual shade of hazel, a hue he had passed on to his daughter. He'd lost his hair at an early age; in fact, Antigone couldn't remember ever seeing a photo of her father with hair. Annaliese's sleek bob, on the other hand, was that champagne shade that disguised gray effortlessly. Antigone's sun-streaked tresses were nearly the same color. She and her mother came from a long line of well-preserved Southern women, but they looked nothing alike. One was a well-tended English park, orderly, soothing, untouchable, and the other was a wild forest, where woodland spirits and practical woodsmen warred in the deep darkness.

Antigone's mother calmly pushed a cold snout out of the

empty pocket of her gray suede coat. "Are you feeling all right? I mean, with the baby. This is what, your seventh month?"

"Yup. I'm just peachy. Some leg cramps, swollen feet, endless fatigue."

Annaliese tapped a white-tipped French manicured nail against her lips in thought. "When I was seven months pregnant with you, I remember I had the strangest dreams. They were quite beautiful in the beginning, full of handsome Greek warriors, beautiful sirens, and magnificent ships. I must have been teaching *The Odyssey* that semester. I quite enjoyed them until everything started turning into food. Boats became banana splits. The women's flowing cloaks were mounds of mashed potatoes. I was always hungry," Annaliese mused. "Are you famished all the time?"

Antigone nodded.

"I used to order huge meals when I was pregnant and only be able to eat a few bites," Annaliese said.

Henry, studying the deer, said, "Our refrigerator was packed with leftovers and doggie bags. I always had something for lunch the next day."

"The point is," Annaliese continued, "pregnancy does something to your perspective, darling. It makes you think you can take on more than you can chew."

"Ah," Antigone said, understanding. "And you think this book situation might be too much for my plate?"

"Not necessarily," Annaliese said. She had that protective look she gave students who were carrying an impossible course load and just discovering it in mid-semester. "I just don't want it to upset you—at this time in your life."

"Don't worry, Mother, it's just given me a little indigestion, or maybe that was the Greek warship I ate at the Dairy Queen."

"The thing is," Annaliese frowned, "people in these situations—heated situations—seldom take the long view."

Henry nodded. "The historical perspective."

Annaliese said, "They're afraid of ideas. They don't want to let them out of the bag because then how will they control them?"

"Control is the main diet of the Mercy Study Club," Antigone said.

"Well, I don't blame you for not wanting to eat at their table," Henry said. "The whole thing gives me the heebie-jeebies. People having to watch what they read, what they say, what they think."

"You were right to challenge them," Annaliese said. "Although I imagine the Thornes don't agree."

"I've been avoiding any deep intellectual discussions with Marian."

"That's my wise daughter." Absently pulling her sleek coat away from Fancy's nibbling lips, Annaliese caressed Antigone's cheek. She tugged the coat closer and shivered. "Temperature's dropping. I'm going in. There's a chapter I want to finish before diving into William's gastronomical explorations. Don't stay out here too long, you two. You'll catch your death."

Antigone nodded. She watched her mother gingerly cross the yard, her high heels wobbling on the uneven ground, her long legs as beautiful as ever. Out of courtesy, as a guest in her daughter's home, Annaliese would be on time for dinner. This was not always the case when Antigone was growing up. Sometimes her parents forgot about dinner completely, unable to tear themselves away from their books, from the words and ideas of strangers long dead. When she was young, Antigone fantasized about snatching the books that held her parents' attention when she could not, those books full of words that would always defeat her. She would grab them out of her parents' hands and fling them into the fireplace. But every time the same thing happened in her daydream: The books put out the fire.

Now, anxiously awaiting being with her own child, Antigone realized that while she had often been jealous of books, she also had prized them. They pictured so prominently in the wonderful moments in her life—the times her mother or father had stretched out on the bed beside her, shoulder to shoulder, and read to her. She could almost hear them. Her mother whispering of a little girl all alone in an orphanage in Paris. Her father chuckling at the antics of a curious monkey.

"You know," Henry said, as the deer searched the ground for remnants of apple. "I kind of like William's cooking." William with his kick-ass cobra tattoo—"the result of one helluva bender in Calcutta"—claimed to put the spirit of India into every dish at the O. Henry Café.

"He's good all right," Antigone smiled. "He's my self-appointed nutritionist."

"I'm glad he takes care of you."

"All the men in my life take care of me."

For as long as she could remember, Henry had liked to tell his daughter jokes. He skewed toward the math jokes, of course, like "What did the zero say to the eight? Nice belt." When he didn't have a joke, he always had a quote. Today was no different.

Henry tucked his hands in his coat pockets and offered an elbow and another quip to his daughter. "Since we have books on the brain, I think Groucho Marx is in order."

"Yeah? What did he say?"

"He said, 'Outside a dog, a book is man's best friend. Inside a dog, it's too dark to read.'"

Antigone's lips curved, as she took her father's arm. They leaned against each other, slowly making their way across the yard. Softly, she heard Henry say, "Your mother and I are proud of you, you know. What you've done here, in this town, the new life you are bringing."

Antigone swung toward her quiet father in surprise. She would have stopped, but he kept pulling her along. "I always considered myself something of a disappointment as an academics' daughter," she said.

Her father ignored the remark. "Remember how I used to measure you when you were small?"

"Notches on the door frame in the library."

"The marks are still there. I thought if I could get the statistics down I could figure you out."

"And did it help?" she asked.

Henry held the gate open for his daughter and then shook his head sheepishly. "You're still a mystery to me, but then I'm a man who likes mysteries."

Antigone squeezed his arm.

Together they made sure the gate was secure before going into the house.

It was a Thanksgiving Day like no other for Ryder. Suddenly, the house was bursting with strangers. He'd been demoted to the living room couch with a sleeping bag. The Browns were situated in his room, while the Thornes occupied the other spare bedroom. Marian Thorne looked at Ryder, as if he might mug her on the way to the bathroom at night. Jonas Thorne was determined to lasso Ryder into watching the Thanksgiving Day football games with him. Ryder thought football was for jerks like Art Junior. The Browns seemed decent enough except they were always talking about books and ideas and stuff.

As he helped the men wrestle with the leaves of the dining room table, he heard the sounds of the Thanksgiving Day parade on the television and thought of his sister Angela. On their final Thanksgiving together, he'd taken her to the Macy's Parade, bundling her up against the November cold and holding her high on his shoulders. She'd squirmed in delight and waved at the giant balloons tethered above the crowded streets of New York. Ryder could still hear her giggles, still feel her small hand patting his head in happiness.

After the parade, he had taken Angela for a real Thanksgiving dinner at the Salvation Army—not the grilled cheese and potato chips his mother thought they ought to be thankful for. Angela had charmed everyone at the soup kitchen, from the smelly old guy seated next to them to the volunteers, mostly white people from the suburbs in their neatly pressed chino weekend slacks and ugly handwoven holiday sweaters decorated with autumn leaves and weird-looking vegetables.

There were rules about Thanksgiving dinner at the Salvation Army. Each plastic plate held out by often dirty and trembling hands received *exactly* two slices of turkey, a plop of stuffing, a pile of green beans, a wiggle of cranberry sauce, and a roll. The stuffing server fashioned a dip in the stuffing. The gravy server filled it with gravy, sometimes smothering the entire plate with the brown sauce. Pumpkin pie and ice tea were distributed at separate tables.

With her warm smile, his three-year-old sister had incited mass benevolence among the servers and her fellow diners. The volunteers, spooning out helpings from pots big enough to carry Angela in, gave them extra turkey and stuffing. One old guy sitting next to them shoveling stuffing into his mouth insisted Angela have his roll: "Watching my carbohydrates," he said. Ryder had cleaned his plate and finished Angela's leftovers. He pocketed both his and her rolls for Angela to eat later.

As the guests left the shelter, they were allowed to take one meal to go—the exact same one they had just been served—already boxed in Styrofoam containers and growing cold. The volunteers, who had been extra-friendly while they were serving, were stubborn about the boxed meals. One meal per person, they said firmly but absently. Their minds were already back in the burbs, where probably a twenty-five-pound bird was spinning in a new rotisserie oven.

"Why can't we give them more?" asked one woman, an aging hippie in macramé jewelry and a tie-dyed dress smelling of incense.

"Because they'll probably just sell it once they get out on the streets," said a woman with sharp manicured nails that nervously played with the gold necklace around her neck.

"So what?" asked the hippie.

A man wearing a Rolex and tassel loafers leaned across the hippie to hand over a box. "If we give them too many, other street people might be tempted to steal from them. Too much could get them into a fight, perhaps stabbed or murdered. This is for their own good."

Angela had politely thanked the hippie then and, pointing to her macramé necklace, said, "Pretty." When the others weren't looking, the woman slipped an extra container in Ryder's hand. He nodded his thanks.

Ryder had tried to keep the dinners for Angela and make them last a few days, but one of the Boyfriends cleaned them out after smoking a couple of joints. Ryder found him, big head in the refrigerator, and said, "Get the fuck out of there. That's for my sister."

Without a word, one big paw filled with stuffing, the doper turned toward Ryder and smacked him with the other paw so hard he flew across the room.

Ryder's mother came running from the bedroom and immediately began to soothe the Boyfriend. "He don't mean nothin', baby." She glared at Ryder, that don't-mess-this-up-for-me look he knew so well. He shrugged and wiped his busted lip.

THEY SAT DOWN TO Thanksgiving dinner—Antigone, Sam, Ryder, Mr. and Mrs. Thorne, the Professors Brown, William, Star, and her mother, Earthly Sims. They studied the table. In the center was William's tofu turkey shaped not in the traditional turkey position, breast up with knobby legs sticking in the air, but like a wild gobbler strutting through the woods in full plumage.

William did the carving with a running commentary on the side dishes. "To begin with, we have pumpkin soup, rich in fiber and beta carotene and good for the eyesight…"

"Pumpkin soup?" whispered Jonas.

Marian shushed her husband.

"But Marian, I like my pumpkin in pie, not soup. I can't eat *orange* soup."

Marian gently stabbed his thigh with a fork. "Of course, you can. You're a grown man."

"Ouch," Jonas said, rubbing his leg.

William ignored the whispering from the Thornes' end of the table. "We have Earthly to thank for the pumpkin soup."

Jonas avoided looking at Earthly.

"One of my Thanksgiving holiday favorites," William continued, "a dish that really takes me back to those Pilgrim days, is the acorn squash stuffed with fruit. Our friend Annie at the apple orchard sent this squash my way. Thank you, Annie."

"Thank you, Annie," concurred Star.

"We've got warm sweet potato salad made by Antigone, a carrot and zucchini puff, and Annaliese and Henry's peanut butter raisin bread. And for dessert," everyone held their breaths, "hot fudge sundaes courtesy of the Thornes."

"Well, of course," muttered Jonas, "we couldn't have pumpkin pie; that was already in the soup."

Marian shot her husband a look, then turned to smile brilliantly at the rest of the table. As everyone began passing serving dishes in various directions, she said over the clicking of silverware, "So, Antigone, what are you going to name the baby?"

"We haven't thought about that yet," Antigone said, handing Sam the squash.

"I think you should name her something pretty," said Star, snagging a slice of bread as it went past.

"It might be a boy, dear," Marian said. "The Thornes have strong Y chromosomes."

"Oh, no, it's a girl," Star said with confidence.

"How do you know?" Marian frowned.

"I just know," Star said, talking around a mouthful of squash. "She's going to be the most beautiful baby any of us have ever seen. And we're all going to love her so much we'll just sit around and look at her. I think we should name her Daisy or Sunbeam."

"That's a toaster," Marian said.

"So?" Star raised an eyebrow.

"Well, you can't name human babies after household appliances."

"Why not?" Ryder asked.

Star giggled, and Ryder winked at her.

Marian cleared her throat with authority. "Well, I always say consult the Good Book. That's where we found Samuel's name. You could do worse than a good Old Testament name."

"There are many wonderful names in mythology and literature, such as Antigone," Annaliese said, casting a smile toward her daughter.

"All those mythological names are the names of heathens," Marian argued, turning to Antigone. "No offense."

"None taken," Antigone said.

"The Greek gods were gods," Annaliese said.

"Not in my neck of the woods," Marian muttered.

THE CALL CAME AS William was pushing seconds. The Thornes exchanged glances of relief. Saved by the bell. "I'll take another serving. Eating for two," Antigone said, as she rose to answer the telephone on the fourth ring.

It was Dash Morgan from the newspaper. After several minutes, she returned to the table.

One look at her and Sam was out of his chair. "What is it?" He took her arm and guided her to her seat. "Tigg, are you all right?"

Silence fell on the room.

Suddenly, Antigone felt about fifty pounds heavier. The tiredness dragged at her spirit. "That was Dash at the paper. The review committee made its decision last night. Four to three to return the books to circulation."

"That's great!" Star smiled.

"Superintendent Mitchell has decided to ignore the committee's recommendation. He refuses to return the books."

"Why would he do that?" Annaliese asked, puzzled.

Sam answered, his eyes still intently watching his wife, "Pressure. Bradford Mitchell wants a new football field. The Mercy Study Club can get it for him."

Antigone sat back and listened to the roar of opinions that filled the vacuum created by Dash Morgan's news, the review committee's recommendation, and the superintendent's spinelessness. The Thornes applauded the superintendent and the Study Club, while the Browns were appalled at their actions.

"We need leaders with strong ideals," Jonas said. "This Mitchell guy could be the next Newt Gingrich or George W."

"The man's an idiot," Annaliese said. "He makes Neanderthal look like Einstein."

Sam said, "Let's talk about this after dinner."

Everyone ignored him.

"Well, I for one, think this town is showing some guts. All this hogwash about freedom." Marian sniffed. "There's freedom, and then there's freedom."

"You mean, your definition of freedom is correct," Annaliese said. "And everyone else's is wrong. Literature is our past, present, and future—all rolled up in one. Would you erase whole parts of our past by denying them? Next thing you'll tell me that you don't believe the Holocaust happened or that they were right in changing the facts of history to make a Smithsonian World War II exhibit politically correct."

"History is up for interpretation," said Jonas.

"That's true as we learn more every day," Annaliese said, "but history *happened*. It cannot be sanitized."

William, who'd sailed to ports in about every autocratic country in the world, rose and began clearing the table. "The first thing dictators do is revise history."

The Thornes did not appreciate comparing good old common sense to totalitarianism and stormed from the table. The Browns exchanged glances and excused themselves with a pat on Antigone's shoulder. Soon Antigone and Sam heard the voice of a football announcer crackling in the other room. Star pulled Ryder outside. Earthly Sims just shrugged and said, "In-laws." Rising, she hefted a stack of dirty dishes. As the former ACLU lawyer swung through the kitchen door, Antigone heard her mutter, "We ought to sue their book-banning butts . . ."

Antigone and Sam sat alone at the table, not touching.

"Well, that's that," Sam said. "Now, life can get back to normal."

CHAPTER 18

UPON A MIDNIGHT CLEAR, A BIBLIOTHÈQUE WAS BORN

I T WAS DECEMBER, A week since Superintendent Mitchell had ignored the review committee's recommendation. Antigone had sunk into a depression that not even the baby's playful kicking could lift. She was entering her eighth month, grouchy, and tired of people insisting on doing things for her. She could tie her own boots, thank you very much, and take care of her deer. She wanted everyone to just leave her alone.

At the back of her mind, the events of the past months worried at her like dripping water on stone: She had told the whole town her secret and for what? Nothing. What should she do now?

She pulled on Sam's barn jacket. Being near the deer would

make her feel better. As she opened the front door, she found Ryder's friend, Ben, and another boy on her doorstep.

"Can we talk with you for a minute?" Ben asked.

Antigone eyed the boy, then Ben. She stepped back and motioned them into the house.

The boy was younger than Ben, maybe thirteen, with gangly arms and legs and pants tugged low on his boney hips by a huge chain snaking from a belt loop to a wallet and a clutch of keys shoved inside one baggy pocket. Antigone could see the tops of the boy's baby blue striped boxers. His dark hair spiked out at all angles, and he seemed to be unaware that the fingers on one hand were tapping relentlessly on his leg.

"Marshall wants to use your library," Ben explained.

"Use it?" Antigone was confused.

The boy called Marshall twisted his body and seemed to glide closer to her. He scanned the room, his eyes shifting from left to right in a face that had an innocent, rubbery quality. "I heard you're getting some cool books, and I, like, *devour* information," he whispered.

"Is he for real?" Antigone asked Ben.

Ben smiled. "Marshall likes to know things: quantum physics, energy, computer technology." He stepped closer and placed a reassuring hand on her shoulder. "Marshall's a good guy. He's smart. I told him about this place because we're starting to get some pretty unusual stuff in here that he might find interesting."

As more and more kids brought books to Antigone for safekeeping, the house and café had taken on the feel of a maze. She glanced at the books piled in stacks along the walls of the living room, the bookshelves long since filled. She supposed she could have said no to the children and their bags of books, but what do you say to a kid who's afraid his parents are going to take exception to his *Harry Potter* collection?

Ben pressed her. "Marshall just likes information—on the Net or in a book. It's not like he's going to research how to build a bomb or something."

Antigone looked startled, and Marshall held up a hand. "No bombs, I promise. Bombs are so, like, loud. I just want to see what you have."

As Ben and Antigone watched Marshall poke around, she said, "I still can't believe all this." She motioned to the stacks. "I thought kids spent all their time staring at screens—computers, e-readers, televisions. I thought books were so—yesterday."

Ben said, "Marshall's on the computer night and day, but books are his best friends."

Seeing the absorbed Marshall, sitting Indian style on her living room floor with opened volumes balanced on both knees and on the floor around him, she had to agree. He flitted from one book to another like a hummingbird. He was so at home and so happy, his busy fingers tapping, tapping.

After a bit of flitting, Marshall settled on two books—one on political history and one on science. "Could I, like, borrow these?" he asked.

And that's when it hit Antigone. Who needed the Mercy High School library? She had one right here. Kids could read whatever they wanted. Everyone would be on the honor system. It would decrease the number of books she was tripping over, and it would drive Irene and the Study Club crazy. Antigone's lips curved. The baby kicked. Who would have thought that she would end up a librarian? She turned to Marshall, "Take whatever you want. Just take care of them." After all, she was still Henry and Annaliese's daughter.

"I'll guard them with my life," said Marshall with a salute.

Three days later, he returned and brought a friend who borrowed three books. The friend also left a grocery bag of his own books, plus several from his dad's shelf of Civil War history books.

And so it began. An underground library. When Sam complained about all the strange children slipping in and out of the house, Antigone moved the library to the vacant building she owned beside the O. Henry Café. At one time a law office, it had plenty of bookshelves. The office and café shared a wall and connecting door, which became the library entrance so William the cook could keep an eye on the comings and goings. Sam, Ryder, and Ben moved the books. Star dusted and organized. Even with so many shelves, the room soon took on the look of Antigone's house with stacks growing from the floor.

Star insisted that everyone who brought a book write his or her name in it. "They ought to be able to take them back when they want," she said. "And if we don't know who a book belongs to, what do we do? We've got three stacks of *Harry Potters*."

As a final touch, Star painted a sign and William nailed it above the door to the library. It said: Our Bookhenge.

There was a steady stream of children—and books—traveling through the O. Henry Café that December. While the rest of Mercy chained holiday wreaths to their doors and cursed contrary Christmas tree lights, Bookhenge exploded in a spirit of giving. No one kept track of the books; no one supervised what someone else read; no one mutilated the books they didn't like or agree with; no one plucked the words they found distasteful from the pages with razor blades. There was something pristine about the library Antigone built, something that shone like a beacon that child after child followed to a new land.

And each time Antigone watched a child walk out the door, clutching a book to his or her chest, she felt like throwing her arms in the air and whirling around until she was dizzy. Her happiness was heady—all mixed up with the children's joy, her reluctant evolution into a librarian, and the satisfaction of outmaneuvering Irene. "Take that, you pie thrower," she said.

CHAPTER 19

FOOD FOR THOUGHT

NOTHING WAS GOING AS Irene Crump had planned. The members of the Mercy Study Club, the school's temporary librarians, grumbled about the boredom, the hours, the rudeness of the few students who still used the school library. Most of the students preferred Antigone's library, which was another thorn festering in Irene's side. "That detestable library is undermining everything," Irene told her husband.

"It's a classic example of women making a fuss over something that isn't of the slightest importance," Arthur said, snapping open the paper to the sports section and pushing aside a ruffled pillow. He was finishing breakfast at the kitchen banquette.

"Thanks for your support." Irene made a face at him.

Not looking up, he said, "What did you expect? It's forbidden fruit. You and your lists have made those books as tempting as free porn."

Irene puffed up, stiffened her spine, and was about to set her husband straight when the phone rang. It was a club member in hysterics because she found a book on the banned list under her daughter's bed along with a well-worn baseball mitt, a slice of pizza, and a rhinestone tiara. "I was looking for dirty underwear and found a dirty book," said the angry club member, who then lowered her voice. "It's that Blume book, for gawdsakes. *Forever.* I thought we got rid of that one. My twelve-year-old baby has been reading about birth control and masturbation, Irene. What good is what we're doing if they're getting this stuff anyway?"

Irene had already had one loud and unpleasant discussion with Superintendent Mitchell about Antigone and her books. The man was useless in a real crisis, as most men were, in Irene's opinion. He hid behind school policy and boundaries: "What can I do, Irene? My authority ends with school property."

Irene was so tired of dealing with idiots, as Arthur put it. Her days were consumed with reassuring those who agreed with her and battling those who did not. Gazing around her, at her beautiful kitchen, the room she loved, with everything exactly where she wanted it, she wished she could stay here forever and never step foot in another library or handle another book or talk with another "concerned citizen." Her kitchen was an appliance paradise with all the latest culinary gadgets plus small custom-made refrigerators strategically concealed in drawers and cabinets so Alice could grab a juice box on her way to soccer or Arthur could pluck a carton of cream for his morning coffee without leaving the banquette. The walk-in pantry was so large that Irene often forgot what was in it. One day while organizing the pantry, Cecily discovered nine bottles of ketchup. She heard Cecily mutter, "What does anyone need with nine bottles of ketchup?"

In her kitchen, butcher block cutting boards slid from hidden places so that wherever she was, Irene could chop up a storm. On that Saturday morning, she needed every one of them. Arthur had informed her over breakfast that someone had made an offer on their house, on this sunny, beautiful kitchen; on her darling solarium; on her shower with the gold fixtures that bombarded and massaged her with hot water from every angle.

"I'm going to build you the house of your dreams, honey," Arthur said full of smiles.

"*This* is the house of my dreams." Irene looked at him.

"We're going to make a bundle off this, Irene. I'm telling you that Japanese couple is gaga over the place." Arthur sniggered. "They didn't even haggle. I threw out some wild, you-wouldn't-believe price and they bit. Some people just have too much money."

"But I *love* this house," Irene said.

"It's just a house!"

"It's our home."

"I've got some great ideas for the new place. How about a fountain in the foyer? Like one of those Italian villas with statues of angels. We could even put real goddamn fish in the fountain. What are they called?"

"Koi."

"Yeah, koi."

As her happy husband banged out the back door, headed for the golf course, Irene began pulling vegetables from the crisper.

WHEN ARTHUR RETURNED FOUR hours later, Irene was still slicing and dicing—and arguing with Art Junior. The counters were piled with chopped lettuce, cabbage, tomatoes, squash, peppers, radishes, cucumbers, and onions. Everywhere Irene looked was salad out of control.

Still, she attacked more vegetables. Her professional chef's knife probably could have sliced lead pipe, so bell peppers were no match for it. As she sliced and slashed with fury, Art Junior turned to his father and whined, "The Jeep doesn't have any power, Dad. I'm gonna take it in to Sam."

"Like you need more get up and go," Irene muttered.

Arthur snagged a pepper slice and popped it in his mouth. "All right, son. Put it on the tab."

"I don't want him taking the Jeep to Sam."

"Why not?" Arthur stared at Irene, shocked. "Sam takes care of all our vehicles."

"Not anymore," Irene said.

Art Junior stole a radish from the cutting board. "She's mad about this library thing. I think it's dumb. Who cares about some old books? Sam's the best," he said, ignoring his mother. "I'll take it to Sam."

"You do and you're grounded." Irene whacked a head of cabbage in half. "Again."

"Are you nuts?" Art Junior exclaimed. "Dad, do something!"

Arthur nodded toward the door. "I'll handle your mother."

Art Junior and his father exchanged smug looks.

"I saw that!" Irene said.

"Women!" Art Junior grumbled, grabbing a soda and slamming the back door.

Arthur pulled a Michelob from one of the refrigerators. "Irene, you don't understand about machinery. Sam's got a sixth sense about mechanical stuff. I'm not putting all my equipment in the hands of an idiot, just because you got a bee in your bonnet."

"And I'm telling you, if you so much as take a riding lawnmower to Sam's Garage, I'll-I'll . . ." Irene exploded, grabbing armloads of chopped vegetables and flinging them at her husband. Arthur froze then slowly pulled a julienne radish from the top of his head. He watched her warily as she waved the chef's knife in front of his nose. Finally, it too rocketed from her hand and stuck in a nearby chopping board, point down, vibrating. He winced.

"And I am *not* leaving my home, Arthur Patrick Crump. But you can. You can do whatever you want," she said, "but you do it alone."

Arthur dropped the can of beer in the sink. It sprayed all over him. "How'd we get from salad to divorce?"

"Somewhere at the radishes, I think." Irene lifted her nose and waltzed from the room.

CHAPTER 20

WHISPERERS WIN

THE WOMAN BESIDE ANTIGONE panted, winked at her, and kept on panting. She was young; this was her first baby, too. Her husband coached her as if he were channeling his inner Vince Lombardi, barking out encouragement about winning and scoring and working hard—and all he had to do was hold her hand. She smiled at Antigone.

"Having a football player?" Antigone asked between pants.

"Quarterback, he says." The woman nodded toward the man behind her.

Her husband frowned. "Focus here, darling. Remember, we're going for the biggest touchdown in life."

The woman and Antigone exchanged grins.

This was the weekly Lamaze class. It epitomized how difficult—and complicated—life had become for Antigone and

Sam since Antigone opened Bookhenge. There were couples who approached them at the refreshment table and offered support for Antigone and the library. And then there were couples who refused to make eye contact and made a point of distancing themselves, edging their exercise mats away from Antigone and Sam. Even the leader, a bubbly young nurse from the hospital, felt the tension; she was decidedly flat by the time the parents-to-be rolled up their mats and stepped out into the January night.

"Everyone be sure to come next week," called the leader as they trudged out. "We're watching a movie—real footage of an actual birth. It's a blockbuster."

Walking into the house, Sam flung his baseball cap on the kitchen counter. "Well, that was fun," he said sarcastically. Seeing Antigone floundering to get her arms out of her coat, he helped her. "Stop struggling."

Antigone huffed. Every stitch of clothing—pulling it on and taking it off—was an ordeal for a body eight months pregnant. Her stomach bumped against Sam as he gently divested her of one of his old winter coats, an ugly example of outerwear that was the only thing she could button. It smelled of him, and when all of this became too crazy, she stuck her nose against the soft wool and inhaled great whiffs of sanity, safety, and Sam.

"I can't help it that people are small minded," she groaned and slowly lowered her aching back into a kitchen chair. "These are people I've known ever since I moved to Mercy. Friends. Customers."

Sam warmed two cups in the microwave—instant coffee

for him and hot chocolate for her. Antigone absently rubbed her back. The phone rang. As he reached for it, Antigone said, "Why bother?"

It was the usual—heavy breathing, whispers in the night, ugly words. "You're the pervert, buddy," Sam said, punching the off button.

Ryder rolled in and slouched against the counter. "Another hater?"

The obscene calls had started shortly after the school board meeting, and now they received at least one a night, sometimes more. Afraid the calls would further upset Antigone, Sam and Ryder leaped to answer the phone at home. William took all calls at the café.

"Nut jobs." Sam pushed the hot chocolate toward Antigone and collapsed in the chair opposite her.

"You're probably talking about our friends," Antigone pointed out.

"Not anymore."

Antigone played with the hot chocolate, stirring and not sipping. She rubbed her back. "There are a lot people who agree with me, you know. They stop me on the street or in the café and tell me so. But it seems harder to remember them than to forget the ones who hate me."

"People don't hate you," Sam said. "They're just . . . caught up in all this."

"Haters get off on hate," Ryder said.

"They're afraid of what they don't understand," Antigone said, "of changing things."

Sam leaned toward her. "Honey, is it worth all this?"

Antigone's hand fell from her back. Across the kitchen, she felt Ryder tense.

She stared at Sam. "What are you saying?" she whispered.

"I'm losing customers, Tigg." Sam sipped his coffee. "Arthur has pulled all of his vehicles, the trucks, the backhoes, even the family cars. He represents a hell of a lot of business for us. He owns one of the biggest construction fleets in this part of the state."

Antigone slumped in her chair. "Oh, no."

"He didn't want to do it, he said, but Irene's on a rampage. She threatened to divorce him if he didn't take his business elsewhere. And don't kid yourself. He's an influential man. He can shut us down with a few words to his golf buddies."

"Damn that Irene."

"And I bet if you asked Earthly and William, business is off at the outlet and café, too."

"I never dreamed . . .," she said.

Sam reached for her hand. "Arthur implied he'd be back in a shot if you cooled it."

"Cooled it?"

"Got rid of all these books, and stopped lending them to people."

"Close the library?" Antigone's eyes rounded in shock. "You're siding with them?" she said, untangling her hand from his.

She looked at Ryder. He walked over and touched her shoulder. "Don't do it. Who cares what those bastards think?"

"Stay out of this, Ryder," Sam growled.

"She loves that place," Ryder argued.

"I've got to think about Antigone's health and our baby. I can't take care of them if the bank forecloses on the garage and I don't have a job."

"And the kids depend on it," Ryder said.

"Ryder!" Sam pushed away from the table and rose. Ryder stepped back. "Leave her alone. This is family business."

"And I'm not family," Ryder nodded in understanding.

Antigone flinched. "That's not true. Sam!"

Ryder stilled. When he stood up to Sam, Antigone realized he had grown since coming here. She watched them, and it seemed, to Antigone, that in this sudden face-off, Ryder was hardening before her very eyes. When the transformation was complete, that stranger she hated, City Ryder, was back. "Spit it out, Mr. Big Shot Mechanic," he whispered, steel coating every word.

"You're just a guy passing through." Sam glared at the boy. "Look her in the eye, and tell her you haven't thought about leaving."

"Ryder?"

Ryder avoided Antigone's stare.

"She must have seemed like easy pickings for someone like you," Sam sneered.

"Someone like me?"

"A user. You saw a good deal, and you grabbed it."

"I was doin' fine before she came along, and I can do it again."

"You've grown soft, Ryder." Sam nodded toward the door. "You couldn't make it out there."

"Fuck you!"

"That's your response to everything, isn't it, Runaway Ryder?"

Antigone grabbed Sam's arm. "Sam, stop it!"

"I don't have to put up with this shit." Ryder whirled, stomped to the door, and grabbed his coat from the hook on the wall. "I'm outta here."

"Good!" Sam shouted.

Antigone struggled to stand. She pushed against the table. "Ryder, wait!"

Ryder stopped with his hand on the doorknob and looked back at her. "Antigone, I . . ." And then he was gone.

The slam of the kitchen door was like a shot, and Antigone raced to the door. Flinging it open, she started after him only to be held back by Sam's arms wrapped around her. "No!" she cried, struggling. "Go after him."

Ryder was no longer in sight. The cold January night had swallowed him up. Sam tugged her back into the house and shut the door. "It's freezing out there. You don't even have a coat on."

"We can't just let him go." Antigone turned in his arms, fists balled against his chest. "Sam, please."

"He'll be back."

She couldn't believe Ryder was gone. Somehow since that day on a deserted road when he'd chewed her out for trusting him, he'd become hers. He'd become family, as much as the child kicking inside her. She pushed Sam away. When Sam reached for her again, pleading, "Tigg," she held her hand up.

"Don't touch me."

She turned away and lumbered down the hall and up the stairs to bed.

Moments later, she appeared at the top of the stairs. She threw a pillow and blanket down at her husband. They glared at each other. "So that's the way it's going to be?" Sam shouted. Antigone folded her arms above her big belly. He hurled the linen toward the couch and pointed a finger at her. "You're gonna miss me. You don't like to sleep alone."

"I'll manage!"

And she did, until the early morning, when she shuffled downstairs, wrapped an afghan around her, and settled down on the floor by the couch. She laid her head next to Sam's. She was almost back to sleep when she felt herself being lifted, carried up the stairs, and tucked gently into bed. She relaxed into Sam's warmth. She felt a breath near her ear, one word: "Sorry."

CHAPTER 21

WISH UPON A PENNY FORK

RYDER FELL QUICKLY BACK into old patterns of survival that had once been second nature. He sought the shadows. He walked in silence and listened with senses so alive he was buzzing inside. He avoided the company of humans. But he was uneasy living that way now. Something was missing. Some edge he used to have was gone, and he lived in terror of screwing up, of looking the wrong stranger in the eye, of falling asleep in the wrong place at the wrong time. He felt unprepared for unpredictability. And on the wild side, the unplanned was the only constant in life.

He'd been on the road for four days. After leaving Antigone's, he hitchhiked south seeking to escape the numbing cold—in the air and in his heart. He'd failed to plan his grand exit well; he had not snatched up gloves or a hat as he blasted from the warm house. He hadn't taken any of his stuff: the seashell Star had given him, the book bag Antigone had bought him, his phony birth certificate. He had gone over the scene in his mind again and again. He should never have let Sam goad him into losing it. Anger was a stupid emotion. And if there was anything Ryder hated, it was being stupid. Stupid people didn't last long in his world.

January was cold even in the South. He hadn't expected that. And he was hungry. He kept to the back roads, gravel and dirt trails like the ones where Antigone had taught him to drive. He accepted rides from poor black farmers in rusted-out old pickups. He trusted them more than the rednecks who reminded him of Art Crump Junior barreling through the countryside as if they owned the place. He watched them from the woods, holding his breath, as they spit gravel and drunken laughter, flying down the road.

Ryder stood near the edge of the woods, deep and shadowy. Spread before him was a brown field, the tobacco long harvested. In the middle of the field, perhaps a hundred feet away, was a thicket, and in the middle of the thicket was an old oak, its limbs spreading out like scarecrow arms. And under the oak was a beacon of light, a campfire, small and bright. He stared at the fire with longing. For the past hour, as dusk came on, he'd studied the man hunkered over the fire. He watched the man pull a dead rabbit from a cloth bag, gut and skin it with the flick of a wrist, and ram it on a spit. Now, it was cooking over the fire along with two cans with crude wire bent for handles. They hung from each end of the spit, sandwiching in the turning rabbit carcass.

In one, the man poured water and beans. In the other, he boiled plain water. The smell of coffee wafted from a pouch lying on the ground by his boot. Throughout all of these efficient and precise chores, the man's back was to him, so Ryder nearly jumped when the man shouted, without turning, "Want some?"

Ryder froze. He didn't answer.

"I got plenty, if'n you're hungry."

"How do you know I'm here?" Ryder asked, remaining by the tree.

"'Cause, boy, I got eyes in the back of my head. Don't you?"

Ryder assessed the man, the location, the cold, and his growling stomach. It was worth the risk. He could outrun the guy if things turned bad. Slowly, he approached the warm fire. His body heat seemed to pour out of his wet kicks, and his cold toes felt like they were going to snap off any minute. He moved with caution, never taking his eyes off the man, who continued to cook dinner. Ryder squatted on the opposite side of the fire. He splayed his hands and stretched them toward the heat.

The man was big, powerful, with massive hands and shoulders. He was darker than Ryder, nearly the color of coal. He seemed to find Ryder's precautions amusing and let out a huge laugh. Ryder jumped. The man's face, which Ryder bet had come up against a number of hard objects in its lifetime, folded into a joyful expression. His deep voice sounded like something you would hear on the radio. Ryder didn't trust him.

"I don't normally eat dinner guests," the stranger assured him with a side glance. "But, I bet you've heard that one before."

Ryder watched his every move. "You could say that."

"Good. It's best not to believe in the kindness of strangers."

Sharing the darkness and aloneness with another human being made Ryder think of the Professor. Of course, Rabbit Man and the Professor were nothing alike. The Professor had insisted there was good in everyone, even sorry bastards like this one. Rabbit Man looked like he'd seen and done some shit in his time, and Ryder didn't want to know about any of it.

The cuffs of Rabbit Man's old Army jacket were dirty and frayed. His pants, now thin and torn, were Army issued, too. His boots were scuffed and muddy, but they looked warm. Rabbit Man wore no gloves and handled even the flame-licked tin cans and steaming rabbit meat with his bare scarred hands. Wrapped around his neck was a bright orange knitted scarf.

Across the fire, Ryder saw something sparkle and leaned closer. A fork poked from Rabbit Man's breast pocket. It was heavy looking, probably solid silver, and fancy. The longer Ryder stared at the fork, the more it captivated him. It glowed in the firelight.

The man deftly sliced a piece of meat from the charred rabbit with a big hunting knife and offered it to Ryder. Ryder hesitated. "Go on, boy. Don't be stubborn or stupid. You know never to turn down food when it's there for the takin'."

Rabbit Man was right. That was one of Ryder's own rules. But he had never eaten a wild thing, a soft creature of the woods, something not found in the day-old section of the supermarket or the dumpster behind a restaurant. It was like watching someone carve up one of Antigone's deer.

"Rabbit's some good eatin'," the man encouraged.

Licking his lips, the hungry Ryder gently pulled the meat from the tip of the man's knife and lowered himself to the ground. He crossed his legs and studied the meat.

"Go on," said Rabbit Man, "you wouldn't want to offend the chef."

Ryder cast a quick glance at Rabbit Man then began to nibble on the meat.

"Well?"

"It ain't a cheeseburger," Ryder mumbled, which caused Rabbit Man to shatter the night with another gleeful roar.

Ryder's last meal had been the morning before. A farmer found some stale cookies in his glove compartment and insisted Ryder take them as he hopped out of the back of the pickup. He thanked the man for the ride and the cookies and watched the truck head toward the interstate. By the time Ryder had walked a mile down the empty back road, the cookies were gone.

Rabbit Man poured half the beans in another tin can and handed the can to Ryder. Ryder imitated the man, who ate the beans by scooping them up with his fingers. As Ryder licked hot juice from his fingers, the fork in Rabbit Man's pocket winked at him.

"I see you lookin' at my fork," Rabbit Man said. "Don't get no ideas about my fork."

"I won't," Ryder said quickly. The can of hot beans burned his hands, but he didn't mind. The heat felt good.

"This here fork ain't for eatin' food. This my penny fork."

"A penny fork?"

"You ain't never heard of a penny fork?" The stranger seemed disappointed in him. He plucked the shiny fork from his pocket and played with it. It reflected the firelight, and Ryder blinked. "You dig out pennies with a penny fork. It's as strong as can be. They don't make 'em like this anymore. Survived the Civil War, World Wars, Vietnam. Hell, I even used this as a weapon in Iraq. Listen to what your mama says, boy, you play with sharp things and you could put an eye out." Rabbit Man stared at the fork, suddenly thoughtful. "Not necessarily your own."

Ryder swallowed and felt his muscles tense. This situation was turning weird. He had about made up his mind to be on his way, when the stranger continued in a lighter tone, "But now, I use this fork only for pennies. Can't help myself. Whenever I'm near a brick wall, I gotta dig out those pennies."

"You find pennies in walls?" Ryder asked.

"Lots of 'em. You know, an old house or old masonry in a garden, they have lots of chinks in 'em. The mortar loosens and crumbles. And people stuff pennies in those cracks in the wall."

"Why?"

"For good luck, boy, for good luck. Those pennies are their wishes."

The stranger offered Ryder another slice of rabbit. Ryder nodded his thanks and chewed the odd-tasting meat as if it were one of William's specialties.

"But why do you dig them out? For the money? Pennies. Don't hardly seem worth it."

Rabbit Man shook his head. "I dig out their wishes and eat 'em and then they become mine."

Ryder choked on the rabbit. "Eat 'em? You eat the pennies?"

"Like candy."

"But why?"

"Because we all need wishes, boy. I don't get sick, and I never have trouble catchin' a rabbit when I'm hungry. If I feel a need to talk, someone like you happens along. I don't freeze at night, and my matches always light, even when they be wet. Undesirables leave me alone. That's because I have all those good wishes inside me."

"How many wishes have you eaten?"

"Thousands probably."

"And they never made you sick?" Ryder asked.

"The wishes haven't. Now the pennies are a different matter. You gotta watch your copper intake, you know."

Ryder slept by the fire that night. Rabbit Man offered Ryder his only blanket, but Ryder declined. "You keep it. I'm gettin' used to the invigoratin' quality of the night air." Invigorating had been one of his vocabulary words in English class.

Rabbit Man laughed. "Invigoratin'. I gotta remember that one."

That night Ryder dreamt of Star. She stood on a hill with her arms stretched to the sky. "Wish on me," she said to him. "Wish on me."

He regretted not saying good-bye to Star. It felt wrong to leave without a word. He should have gone by her house that night and tossed a pebble against her window. He would have liked to have seen her one last time, leaning out the upstairs window, laughing at him, blowing gusts of frost with her warm breath.

He also saw Antigone in his dream. She was in the truck stop where they first ate together. She was asleep, her cheek cradled against her arm on the tabletop. The table was filled with food, more food than three pregnant women could eat. And still the waitress brought more. She balanced a greasy platter of sausages on Antigone's sleeping head and shrugged at him, "She always orders more than she can eat." He wanted to fling the sausages on the floor. Didn't she know Antigone was a vegetarian? The smell alone would kill her.

An owl swept the air just above his head, so low its wings almost brushed his cheek. *Hoo hoo hoo-hoo.* Ryder jolted awake. *Hoo hoo hoo-hoo.* The huge bird settled on a branch of the oak in the middle of the field. Its head swiveled in the moonlight; dark eyes studied him. Its deep voice barked again.

Ryder shivered and inched closer to the fire. The last time he saw the Professor it had been a night colder than this. They'd met up in an alley under the single streetlamp. The Professor preferred a well-lit alley to the shelters, some place he could read one of the books from his precious sack.

That night Ryder had scolded him for trading his gloves for a book.

"Man, you don't know nothin'. Every day you survive, it's a freakin' miracle," he'd said, pulling off his gloves and handing them to the Professor. "Put these on. They got holes, but they're better than nothin'." He leaned down and tugged the layers of sweaters closer to the old man's whiskery chin.

"So what did you get for the gloves?" Ryder asked, settling on the cold concrete next to the Professor, his knees drawn up to his chin. He leaned close, offering his warmth. The gloves had long ago lost most of their fingertips so Ryder could see the Professor's cracked fingers as they caressed the old cloth cover, which was worn in spots and bent at the corners.

"*The Last of the Mohicans.* A bloody good swashbuckler. The hero is named Hawkeye."

"Hawkeye, huh? That's a cool name."

And then the old man nestled into Ryder and began to read. His precise tongue, sharpened perhaps in a fine British finishing school (according to one rumor on the street), carved images and served them up for Ryder's imagination. Time slowed, moving as if in a peaceful dream. Ryder closed his eyes and leaned his head back against the hard brick wall. Words echoed down the silent alley, floating up through the cold darkness, mixing with snowflakes.

Ryder didn't know how long he and the Professor had been asleep when he heard footsteps. Immediately, he was awake and alert. He feigned sleep, however, to find an edge. Ryder always looked for an edge.

The three men who attacked them were after the Professor's bag. They thought it was full of stuff to pawn, perhaps some clothes warmer than theirs, maybe some booze. When a hand reached past Ryder to grab the Professor's moth-eaten sweaters and shirts, Ryder instinctively kicked it. The thief swore, lifted Ryder by the jacket, and flung him across the alley. He slammed into a pile of boxes, the bones in his spine rattling like a child's toy.

While two of them held Ryder, squirming and twisting in their hands, the leader punched the Professor with huge fists, slamming his foot into the pile of human rags again and again, until the old man released his desperate grasp on the sack. Finally, the leader snatched it, looked inside, and then upended it in disgust. Books poured down on the Professor's body.

"Books. Ain't nothin' worth nothin'," said the leader. He grabbed the book from the Professor's limp hand, *The Last of the Mohicans,* and ripped the pages out. He flung them into the air. They snowed down around the Professor. He nodded at one of the other men, who then slammed a fist into Ryder's gut, doubling him over. Ryder dropped to the concrete as the men melted into the night, laughing. He crawled over to the Professor.

Ryder pushed the Professor's sweaters aside with shaking hands and pressed his ear against the old man's chest. It was such a skinny chest, nothing more than loose skin dangling on bones. He heard a slight rattle. "Man, I gotta get you to a hospital," he muttered, pulling the Professor into his arms.

The Professor coughed and sputtered blood.

Ryder was crying now. "You and your goddamn books. I knew some day they'd get us in trouble." He rocked his friend. "Don't you die on me! Not tonight. Professor . . . Professor?" Once again he desperately listened for a precious pounding inside the old man's withered chest. Nothing.

Hadn't Ryder warned the Professor? He wanted to shake the old man and shout: see how quick it can happen, how the world can spin out of control in a moment? Snowflakes came out of the night and drifted down onto the Professor's peaceful face. They caught in his whiskers and sparkled. They dissolved against his chapped lips and mixed with the frozen tears on Ryder's cheeks.

Ryder sniffed, straightened the Professor's sweaters, pulling them tighter. Patting his old friend's chest, he said, "You shoulda kept the gloves, crazy old man."

RYDER DISCOVERED, STARING INTO Rabbit Man's fire, that his cheeks were damp. He immediately wiped them with his sleeve. With a quick glance to the sleeping figure across the fire, he pulled out a wallet that didn't have much in it, just a strip of pictures from one of those photo booths and a folded piece of paper. He slipped them out. He tipped the photo strip so he could see Angela's smiling face by the light of the fire. They'd been happy that day. It seemed like a million years ago. With a gentle stroke over Angela's face, he wished he had a picture of Antigone, too.

Carefully, he returned Angela's picture to his wallet and unfolded the page from *The Last of the Mohicans*. He read it aloud, in the middle of nowhere. "I am on the hill-top, and must go down into the valley; and when Uncas follows in my footsteps, there will no longer be any of the blood of the Sagamores, for my boy is the last of the Mohicans. . ."

Throughout the rest of the night, Ryder dozed only to be awakened by the owl flying overhead, back and forth, calling, always calling. He pulled his jacket closer, trying to get back to sleep. He heard a groan and warily turned his head. Across the fire, Rabbit Man thrashed, fighting some kind of demon in his dreams. A hoot broke the night silence. Suddenly, Rabbit Man sprang upright, his eyes wide open, the hunting knife clutched in his hand. Ryder froze. Tense, he watched Rabbit Man turn toward him.

"Who you be?" Rabbit Man eyed him suspiciously.

The knife glinted in the firelight.

"A dinner guest," Ryder said.

Keeping his eyes on Ryder, Rabbit Man patted the pocket where he kept his penny fork. Still there. "You wanna be my son? I be needin' a boy to take care of me in my old age."

Ryder saw the craziness in Rabbit Man's eyes. His loneliness edged toward Ryder. He saw himself years from now, floating over the land like a spirit, clutching silverware. No Professor to tether him. No Star to make him want to be better. No Antigone to believe in him. He would become a wild thing, living off the land, hunting down rabbits and deer. He knew their ways, how to lure them in. He'd get a knife and . . .

Ryder realized he was kidding himself. He couldn't gut a Bambi. He didn't want to be that man. The Professor had insisted they all had choices. Ryder used to wonder at the Professor's naiveté, like choice was free, like you could just want it and it would be. Could it be true?

"Nah. Can't be your son," he said. "I got family."

Suddenly, Rabbit Man's features smoothed, his shoulders relaxed, and he smiled. It was as if the demons and lunacy of night dreams vanished. Once again, he was the man confidently roasting a skinny carcass in the night glow, laughing at a stranger watching from the shadows. "You missin' out on a BIG inheritance," he said, plucking the fork from his pocket and waving it in the air like a sword.

The eastern sky was shading from gray to purple and gold. Rabbit Man didn't go back to sleep, and neither did Ryder. He watched Rabbit Man pack up his things in the dawn light, fling his dirty drawstring bag over his shoulder, and give him a nod. As the man strode off across the field, his laughing voice carried in the morning quiet: "This here an invigoratin' mornin'."

Ryder waited until he was sure Rabbit Man was long gone and then chose the opposite direction—toward Antigone and home.

CHAPTER 22

INSPIRING MUTINY

THE JANUARY MEETING OF the Mercy Study Club came to order with a growl.

Julie Masterson Clark had sensed the tension in the air the moment Cecily answered the door. Irene's maid simply nodded toward the solarium and high-tailed it back to the kitchen, her shoulders pressed protectively up to her ears. When Julie stepped into the solarium, Irene was pacing and issuing orders. Julie slid into a French Provincial chair and crossed her arms.

"I've canceled this month's regularly scheduled program," Irene said. Club members exchanged glances. "We've got far more important business to discuss. The program schedule will be pushed back one month. Consult your schedules, presenters, and do the math. Julie will deliver her presentation on the new Kennedy book in February; Arabella's Daughter of the Confederacy cookbook will be the March topic, etcetera, etcetera, etcetera."

Most of the members of the Mercy Study Club considered it wisest not to tangle with Irene when she was in a mood. Arabella, who considered herself old enough to do what she liked and say what she liked when she liked, was one of the few willing to face an edgy Irene. "What are you fussing about now, Irene?"

"We need to respond to the situation in this town."

"Situation?" Mary Beth asked.

"Antigone Brown and her library," Irene snapped. "I think it's important that we, as a club and as individuals, be more assertive in the coming days."

"More assertive? My God, Irene, the whole town is at each other's throats," said Julie, to the shock of several members, who were sinking in their seats as if to stay out of the line of fire. "I, for one, think we've gone too far already."

Mary Beth nodded. "I was giving blood the other day at the Red Cross, and the nurse asked me what the hell *we* thought we were doing. She said she never asked me to protect her kids from smut. This was all supposed to be accomplished on the down low. And now I've got Red Cross nurses waving long needles in my face and taking me to task, Irene."

Another member, furious with Antigone's influence over her daughter, said, "She's inspiring wholesale mutiny among our children. One of my favorite biographies is missing. I bet it's in her library. I questioned my little Audrey, and she denied ever seeing the book. But she had that look on her face like she's telling a whopper."

A senior member, who had complained to Julie about still having to volunteer at the school library, said, "Let's be done with this. It's interfering with my golf game."

"People are calling *us*," another member whined. "I don't like strangers calling me."

"My calls are running about fifty-fifty—half in support and half ready to hang us," Mary Beth calculated.

"I've been getting complaints, too." Irene admitted to the room. "But also calls of support. Lots of them. People *do* agree with us. People *do* care about their children."

"Of course, they care, Irene." Mary Beth rolled her eyes. Julie bit her lip to hide a smile. The easily bored Mary Beth abhorred wishy-washy. In her logical world, you took a stand, watched how it went down, reassessed, and adjusted your plan. The point was: get the job done or move on. Don't waste time on lost causes.

Julie felt a surge of strength knowing that Mary Beth was no longer solidly in Irene's camp. This boldness was not entirely new. It had begun to grow a week ago, on the afternoon she'd dropped her daughter Jamie off downtown to do some Christmas shopping. In the rearview mirror, as she pulled away, Julie was shocked to see her daughter look up and down the street and then dash into the O. Henry Café. Curious, Julie parked and watched the café entrance. After about fifteen minutes, Jamie emerged, smiling, holding two books. Two days later, on a school morning, Julie sneaked into the café, heavily layered in a hat, scarf, and sunglasses, and visited Antigone's lending library. She saw two other adults there and was careful not to make eye contact. She was astounded at how many books there were. She found an old romance, one she'd read in high school: *Rebecca* by Daphne du Maurier. It brought back memories of staying up too late on school nights, unable to turn off the light and turn away from the perils of the young wife so in love and so afraid of her mysterious husband.

Standing in that little hole-in-the-wall library, Julie experienced again that rush of feelings that comes with a story that has you by the throat. God, she loved that feeling. And with each moment that passed, each book she touched, she hated even more what the Study Club, *her* club, was doing.

Julie rose from her seat in Irene's solarium. "We need to return those books to the library and end this war."

Irene whirled on her. "Give in to Antigone Brown! H-E-double hockey sticks no," Irene shouted. "She's polluting our children's minds. We should have her thrown in jail."

Arabella stomped her gold-handled cane. "She went too far with that library. My son Braxton could find something to charge her with." Braxton Richey was the county prosecutor.

Seeing the idea take hold in Irene's eyes, Julie cried, "Antigone's not a pornographer. You're insane, Irene." Julie watched Irene tug on her jacket and lift her chin.

Mary Beth made a cut in the air with her hand. "It's going to be damned difficult to prove that a) the books are obscene, and b) Antigone intended to hurt anyone. What you can get away with in a little school library and what you can get away with in a court of law are two entirely different things, Irene. Not to mention the fact that she's pregnant. No jury's going to send a young mother to the slammer over *Huckleberry Finn*."

"We'll see if it sticks or not," Irene, said refusing to back down.

Julie glanced around the room and then took a step closer to Irene. "I'm warning you. You do this, Irene, and come fall, you'll have some competition in the club president election. My grandmother founded this club, and I'm not letting you run it into the ground."

Irene's eyes widened then narrowed. She lifted to her full height and pulled so hard on her jacket Julie was surprised it didn't rip. "Bring it on, Julie."

"I will," Julie said with a smile, turned, grabbed her handbag, and started for the door. The club burst into whispers. Behind her she heard something smack against the French doors. She glanced back. Irene had rocketed a pillow from the loveseat across the room. Her aim was Babe Ruth sure. The panes in the windows rattled, and the mouths of the startled women snapped shut. Irene stared at Julie defiantly and said, "Attention! Now, I want each and every one of you to think about this, to think about your nice homes and your darling children. And you think about all those things that you hold dear being threatened by Antigone Brown. Take charge, ladies, or take cover."

CHAPTER 23

LOCK UP

A NTIGONE SAT ON THE bed Ryder had once slept in and listened to the sleet clicking against the windowpane. As predicted, the winter storm was dipping down into the Carolinas, starting as rain a few hours earlier and now glazing everything it touched with ice. She glanced around the room. She'd washed the linens and folded Ryder's clothes in a neat pile. She'd straightened the textbooks on the desk. Everything was ready for him when he came home. The baby waved, rolling a fist along Antigone's uterine wall. She placed her hand on the moving mound, and her mood swung from anger that Ryder had left her to worry about what he was eating and where he was sleeping. Was he safe in this storm? Yesterday in the grocery store, while other storm-crazed shoppers ransacked the bread aisle and battled over batteries and candles, she stood in the cereal aisle, reaching for extra boxes of Froot Loops and thinking, "Ryder will be starving when he gets home."

She heard the doorbell and immediately thought, "He's back." Pushing herself to her feet, she started for the stairs, making it halfway down by the time Sam opened the door.

"Cody, what are you doing out in this mess?" Sam asked with a grin.

Antigone stopped and clutched the banister. Had something happened to Ryder? Sheriff Cody Dunn was not a usual visitor.

"Hey, Sam." Cody doffed his hat, twirling it nervously in his hands. "Is Antigone here?"

Sam's grin dissolved. "What's this about, Cody?"

Cody looked up, and Antigone descended the rest of the way down the stairs. She automatically reached for Sam's arm.

Cody took a deep breath. "Antigone Brown, I have a warrant for your arrest on charges of disseminating obscene materials."

"The hell you have," Sam snarled.

"What!" Antigone cried.

"Sam, I don't like this any better than you do," Cody said quickly. "You're the last person I want to get on the bad side of. I got tires that need rotating. But once the county prosecutor has issued a warrant, I'm duty bound to serve it. Let's not have any trouble. I'll just take her back to the office, and we'll straighten this out."

"You're not taking her anywhere." Sam stepped between Antigone and Cody.

Cody glanced at Antigone. "Talk to him. Let's do this nice and easy."

Cody was an unusual specimen of small town law enforcement. He had a degree in criminal justice. "Imagine going to school for that," the older residents said. He worked out regularly and watched what he ate. He could pass by the doughnut shop without a glance. He grew up in Mercy, just about defined "ruggedly handsome," and surprised everyone when he came back home to settle down. He talked knowledgeably about DNA testing and, in his off hours, did curls on a homemade skateboard ramp in his backyard. Antigone liked Cody. He was even a vegetarian.

And she didn't want Sam getting into trouble. She pulled Sam around to face her, stepped back and up so she was standing on the first stair, and placed her forehead against his. "It's okay." She kissed him. "Call Earthly."

Sam clutched her tightly to him and nodded. Then he helped her into his old winter jacket, hanging on a hook by the door, and knelt to tug on her boots. He rose and glared at Cody, "I'm coming to get her."

Cody nodded. "I certainly hope so."

As they went out the door, Sam shouted, "You be careful on those roads."

ANTIGONE HAD NEVER BEEN arrested before. On paper, she was a model citizen—not so much as a speeding ticket. She kept all her business licenses current and paid her taxes. She didn't employ illegal aliens. She didn't scam cable channels.

She resisted the urge to tear out coupons from magazines at the obstetrician's office. And she was 99.9 percent sure the sheriff didn't know anything about her trip to Greensboro to purchase the illegal wares of Hector Bob.

So Antigone didn't know what to expect when she was thrown in the slammer. Maybe a stark cell with sliding bars for doors, gruel for food, rats as big as dogs, and lustful inmates. She certainly hadn't anticipated being helped off with her coat, gently lowered in the chair behind Cody's desk, and told to answer the phones. Cody and his deputies had their hands full with the storm. He got her settled and then went back out to pull cars out of ditches and visit homes that had lost power. He moved elderly folks in with neighbors and relatives who had heat and electricity.

Outside, the sleet had already begun to taper; once in a while the day reverberated with the crack of a tree branch tumbling down. Some missed power lines; some didn't. A family of travelers came in and asked for a place to stay. The one motel in town was full so Antigone set them up in one of the offices. They rolled out sleeping bags on the floor, and the two kids, ages five and seven, hauled in their backpacks of toys and books. Antigone called the restaurant and asked William to deliver a big batch of vegetarian lasagna and garlic bread. She kept the coffee pot in the lounge filled.

By evening, the phones were quiet. People were off the roads and home in their beds. Temperatures hovered around the freezing mark. Antigone had talked to Sam several times during the day, reassuring him that she was fine. Now she was beating Cody Dunn in gin rummy, a penny a point, five hundred wins.

Antigone had a sense about cards. She was a natural gambler. She was completely illogical when it came to bidding—an approach to cards that drove orderly Sam crazy. No matter what game he taught her, she usually ended up annihilating him after a few hands.

Cody groaned as Antigone fanned her remaining cards on the table. He dispiritedly began to count the points he'd been left holding in his hand. "I wouldn't worry about it much," Cody said. "Their case is weak. This is more a nuisance than anything. But Braxton Richey has some determined people on his back and he has to make them happy. I wouldn't be surprised if he lets things cool down and then drops the charges."

"I hope you're right."

"You'll see. Your lawyer will carve this case like butter. Probably go after the school system, too. It's what I'd do."

"I just want to get home to Sam."

"I'll be only too happy to hand you over to him. I'm not one of his favorite people right now. And I got that tire situation, as you know." Cody grinned. Antigone started dealing another hand, and Cody looked at his cards and groaned. "What's taking that lawyer so long?"

THE NEXT MORNING ANTIGONE woke on a cot in a cell. The door was wide open, and she walked out into the office. She smelled coffee and cinnamon. In the lounge, she found a spread of breads, rolls, and cereals and a hot plate with dishes of scrambled eggs and hash browns. She smiled. William had already been here. She heard laughter and followed it to one of the offices, where the two boys were sitting on sleeping bags, thumbs flying over electronic game boards in their hands. She made a stop by the rest room, then went looking for Cody.

The day was bright outside Cody's office window. Everything sparkled. The trees were encased with ice, and the sun shimmered down every tree limb and branch. They heard a crack and thump. Cody glanced up from some paperwork and said, "Beautiful, isn't it? Too bad it's such a pain in the butt."

"The ice is already melting; I can hear the dripping," she said, dropping into a chair across from the desk.

"The power company's been working all night. Streets will be navigable in a few hours. Then we'll start getting everybody back where they belong."

IT WAS SHORTLY AFTER noon, and several gin rummy hands later, when Earthly Sims, accompanied by Sam, strode into Cody's office, just about as big and bright as you could get. Antigone had never seen her friend in ACLU, don't-mess-with-me power mode. She wore a peacock blue suit and matching hat with a wide brim that swept across her face and down one side to her chin. The Earthly she knew preferred elastic-waist trousers and roomy tunics that allowed "a woman of comfortable size to breathe." Antigone looked closer; Earthly even wore eye makeup. Antigone's lawyer was armed to her big, white teeth.

"You can turn my client loose," Earthly said, slapping a piece of paper on top of the playing cards on Cody's desk.

"About time you got here," Cody said.

Earthly looked at Antigone. "You're lucky I kept my license in North Carolina current. Star said I might need it."

Cody glanced at the paperwork. "Braxton dropped the charges? That was fast."

"I eat boys like him for breakfast," Earthly said. Earthly had once told Antigone that she was a shark when it came to defending the rights of the downtrodden, bullied, and exploited. The ACLU had been sorry to see her go. "Giving me that 'applying contemporary community standards' crap. I showed him community standards. I dropped a mess of books from Antigone's library on his desk and demanded to know how *any* of those books were obscene. Hell, half of them were his personal favorites. I told him to get his mama under control and get back to catching some real criminals."

Cody laughed.

"That a girl," Antigone said.

"I don't like people who mess with my people." Earthly lifted her chin.

Antigone turned to Sam. She stepped into his embrace. He squeezed her tight. She felt the baby kick and suddenly felt like laughing. Then she pulled away and inhaled sharply. There, standing back from the group, leaning against the door, was Ryder.

"Hey," he said, hoarsely, straightening.

Joy and anger warred inside her. When she didn't say anything, he shifted nervously. "Can't leave you alone a minute. I'm gone a week and you get yourself thrown in jail. Hell, the whole state falls apart. What's with this ice shit?"

She stepped toward him. "You really pissed me off, Ryder," she said.

"I know."

"I was worried sick."

Earthly frowned at him. "And you didn't say good-bye. Star's ready to kill you."

Ryder ducked his head. "Thought as much. Ma'am."

Antigone said, "But Star was sure you'd be back."

"She'd know."

Antigone nodded once. She smoothed her top over her large belly. Sam touched her arm, held her coat open, waiting for her to slip into it. He tugged a wool watch cap over her ears and handed her a pair of gloves. "I'm ready to go home," she said.

"Me, too," Ryder said.

CHAPTER 24

NIGHT VISITORS

S TAR WOKE WITH A start. What had disturbed her? she wondered. She contemplated her room: The ceiling twinkled with glow-in-the-dark stars. Under the window—undisturbed—were all her candles and special boxes, the ones Ryder found so fascinating. He was the only person in the world Star let poke his finger in the sand she'd saved from her first trip to the beach or handle a hodge-podge of items in the boxes: a pretty Canadian dollar bill, a shiny beaded Mardi Gras necklace, a tiny tooth, a valentine from her father, the blue shell from a robin's egg, a pen that wrote in five colors, a chain of paper clips, a red AIDS ribbon.

"Why do you keep this junk?" he had asked.

"They're memories," she'd said, "Don't you have memories you want to keep?"

Ryder had shrugged and looked away.

Now, Star continued to search out the reason for her sudden awakening. She turned to the bookshelf, where stuffed animals were crammed—elbow to paw, tail to shoulder—with books. They looked back at her with serene button eyes. She shoved back the covers and swept to the window in her long flannel nightgown. She stared into the night in the direction of the deer farm. She glanced down the road. She could see no car, hear no engine.

But someone was coming.

Star tiptoed down the stairs and through the kitchen. Stopping at the door, she scrambled into her parka and boots, toppling once when she caught a boot in the hem of her nightgown. Shutting the back door quietly behind her, she cut through backyards and ran to Antigone's house. At Antigone's, she circled around to the front and stopped under Ryder's window. Shivering in the January night, her gasps freezing the air, she flung a handful of pebbles at the window. It took only one try to awaken him; Ryder was a light sleeper.

"What are you doing out there?" Ryder growled, leaning out the window. "And you're in your pajamas. Where the hell are your clothes?"

"There's no time." Star hopped from one freezing foot to the other. "They're coming!"

"Who's coming?"

"I don't know."

"Star, I ain't in the mood for this psychic shit tonight."

"Ryder, please, they're almost here!"

Star and Ryder heard the powerful Jeep engine at the same time. They turned toward the road as the shiny black four-wheeler passed under a streetlamp and stealthily made its way toward the deer farm across the street. The driver had turned out the headlights. They heard laughter inside the Jeep. Ryder was shoving his legs into his jeans before Star could say another word.

"Back door," he commanded.

RYDER QUIETLY MADE HIS way out of the house. He found Star huddled in the azaleas. He had grabbed a jacket and a pair of sweatpants as he left his room, and he shoved the pants at Star. "Put these on," he said as he pulled on his jacket.

"Ryder . . ." Star whined.

"Now. You'll freeze your ass off."

Star quickly pulled on the pants, which ballooned around her skinny legs. Ryder knelt and stuffed the pants into the tops of her boots. Rising, he said, "Now stay behind me, and try not to trip."

They rounded the side of the house, and Ryder pulled Star back into the shadows. He pressed a finger to her lips. The Jeep idled across the street. Then the engine was shut off, and there was silence. More whispers and laughter. When the driver opened his door, the dome light briefly illuminated three boys. One boy held a bundle in his arms.

Ryder and Star watched the boys pace up and down the fence of the O. Henry Deer Farm.

"I don't see them," said one boy.

"They're in there," said another.

The third motioned. "Throw him in. He'll flush 'em out."

In the moonlight, Ryder saw the bundle wiggle and the boy holding it fish out a small white and black spotted dog. Before he knew it, the boy had tossed the dog over the eight-foot fence and in with the deer. "No!" screamed Ryder, racing across the yard. The boys spun around, and Ryder recognized them from the football team. The biggest one was Art Crump Junior. Ryder ran for the locked gate, but before he could reach it, two of the boys tackled him. He automatically began throwing punches, and Star started screaming. This was not going to be like the fight at school. Art Junior didn't mind a little help this time. Ryder was seriously outnumbered in people and poundage.

"Hold him," Art Junior instructed his two beefy friends. Then he slammed a fist into Ryder's gut, forcing the air out of him. The other two laughed and let him drop to the ground. Out of the corner of his eye, he saw Art Junior's boot coming for his head and tried to roll away. It glanced off his temple. From far away, he heard the dog barking and Star sobbing his name over and over. He squinted in her direction, felt blood running into his eye, and saw her struggling with one of the boys. "Don't touch her," he grunted, trying to push himself up to his hands and knees.

Then he saw big hands, Sam's, grab the boy's shoulder and jerk him away from Star. She broke free and ran to him. He felt her hand on his face. He wanted to vomit but not in front of Star. He ducked his head, breathed, and tried to get

up again. Then he heard Antigone's voice telling him everything was going to be all right. He fell back to the ground
and rolled over, peering up at her through an eye already
half-swollen shut. He knew that was a lie. All hell was breaking loose beyond the fence.

As Sam spun the combination on the gate padlock and
shoved it open, he thought about how most people think
of deer as silent creatures striding peacefully along the edge
of a cornfield or leaping through the forest. Few hear them
in distress, scared, screaming that high-pitched half-snort,
half-whinny. He tuned out the frantic deer and tried to get a
direction on the yapping dog. Two security lights along the
fence showed darting shadows and chaos. The mutt, which
had some hunting hound in him, was in his element, chas-
ing the frightened deer and snapping at their heels. The deer
at first moved together, then dispersed in several directions,
each searching for a way to escape. Sam dived for the dog,
but it only growled and eluded him. On the ground, Sam
felt hooves pounding all around him. He saw Antigone begin to enter the compound and yelled, "Stay out of here!"
Sam lifted himself up and again gave chase. He closed in on
the dog, reaching for its scruffy neck, but it dodged away.
He almost had it cornered under one of the spotlights when
he heard a snarl from behind. He turned in time to see an
object hurling through the night. It was the feral cat.

The ferocious blur attacked the dog without mercy. Dog
and cat were about the same size, but the cat fought how

Sam imagined Ryder would—fearlessly, no holds barred, like life depended on it. It swiped, slashed, and ripped, leaving the dog yelping in pain. As quickly as it entered the fray, the cat completed its job. There was silence.

The dog lay on the ground, motionless, one eye gone, its flank sliced open. The cat that had befriended the deer took one last look at its opponent, then slowly turned and disappeared into the night.

"That cat killed my dog!" shouted Art Junior, kicking the fence.

Sam glanced back at the group. Everyone from Antigone, Star, and Ryder to William and Earthly Sims, who'd come running as soon as they heard the uproar, was in shock. "Oh man," said one of Art Junior's buddies. Then Sam heard Antigone moan and saw her start through the gate. He whirled to see where she was going, and his heart caught. Fancy. Panicked, the young deer had thrown itself against the fence with such force that its leg and jaw were entangled in the mesh. Sam sprinted for Antigone, grabbed her arm, and pulled her to a halt before she could reach the injured animal. "Don't go near her. One kick and she could kill you and the baby."

"She's bleeding," Antigone pleaded. "I have to help her."

Still looking into his wife's eyes, Sam started issuing orders: "Earthly, call the vet and Cody Dunn. Star, get some blankets. William, keep an eye on those bastards."

Star and Earthly scattered. Ryder rose from the ground, staggered a moment, then righted himself. He swiped at the blood on his face once then stared at Art Junior. Without saying a word, he passed by the boys, bumping Art Junior's shoulder, on his way to the gate and Antigone. Art Junior took a step toward him, but one of his friends grabbed his arm, saying, "Let's get outta here."

As the boys stepped toward the Jeep, William stood his ground. He tapped a baseball bat against one hand. "Don't move."

"You can't hold us here," Art Junior said.

William let his arm drop, as if by accident, and the bat smashed the Jeep's headlight. Art Junior howled, "That's my Jeep!"

"It's gonna be your head, if you move again," William said.

None of the three boys seemed willing to cross a cook wielding a baseball bat like a ginzu knife. When Earthly returned, William sent her back to call the boys' parents. He silenced the boys' protests with a whack to the hood of the Jeep.

Star ran up and thrust the blankets in Sam's arms and then backed away to where Ryder stood, watching intently. Antigone and Sam slowly approached Fancy.

"Sam!" Ryder warned.

Sam glanced back at the boy. "I got it."

Sam hovered nearby ready to jerk Antigone to safety at the first sign of distress from the deer. Antigone whispered to Fancy. She stretched out her hand, walking nearer and nearer. The animal snorted and flailed. Sam and Antigone stopped. When Fancy settled down, they began approaching her again. She was caught, the steel wire of the chain link fence cutting into the deer's leg and jaw. Blood dripped from cuts on her flank, legs, and snout. Angling away from the dangerous hooves, Antigone laid a hand on the deer's quivering neck. "It's going to be okay," she whispered. "Shhhh. It's going to be okay." Fancy grew calm. Sam reached around Antigone and gently draped a blanket around the trembling animal.

"She's going into shock," he said, but he doubted Antigone heard him. The night was quiet except for the heavy breathing of the deer and Antigone's whispers. Leaning toward the deer, she was singing the alphabet song like a lullaby.

WHEN ARTHUR AND IRENE arrived, the other two boys were in the back of Cody Dunn's squad car, crying. Irene spotted Art Junior, arguing with Cody. "This is bullshit; I'm outta here," said Art Junior, starting for the Jeep. Cody grabbed his arm, spun him around, and started handcuffing him. Art Junior struggled. "Hey, get off me!"

Irene barely waited for Arthur to stop the car before she jumped out and ran to her son. Arthur was right on her heels.

"What are you doing?" she cried.

"Cody, what's going on here?" Arthur frowned.

"These boys trespassed, assaulted another individual, and endangered an animal. I'm taking them in, Arthur."

Arthur demanded to know what happened. Art Junior told them everything. He didn't even try to lie. In fact, he was proud of himself. His father stepped in front of him. "What the hell is wrong with you?"

Art Junior sneered. "She's a troublemaker. Mom said so."

"I never!" Irene gasped.

"You said she was ruining everything, her and that stupid library. That's all you talk about!"

Arthur grabbed his son's arm. "Don't use that tone with your mother."

"I'm tired of this crap, and I'm tired of her," Art Junior said, nodding toward Antigone. He shrugged out of his father's hold. "She got what she deserved."

"This is the stupidest damn thing you've ever done," Arthur said.

"What's the big deal?" Art Junior groused. "It's just an animal. Their stupid cat killed my dog, and you don't see me crying like a baby."

Irene studied her son with sadness. How had it come to this? she wondered. She spent all her time fighting people—the son who had become a stranger to her; her husband who wanted to sell their home; her friends and neighbors who couldn't understand that she was doing everything for them, for the good of their children and community. She imagined what her mother would say about a grandchild landing in jail. No one in her family had ever been incarcerated, except a distant cousin whom her mother had refused to talk about. "We do not entertain Cousin Alf in this house," she'd said the one year Irene, age eight, had asked to invite him to Thanksgiving dinner.

Irene turned away from her son in disgust. She watched Antigone stroking the deer's neck. Suddenly, she flung open the gate and ran over to Antigone and Sam. Cody chased after her.

"Irene, come back here."

"Antigone! Please don't press charges against my boy."

A furious Sam stepped between Antigone and Irene. "Hell, yes, we're pressing charges."

"But he's my son."

"He's an out-of-control, self-centered prick . . ."

But he's my prick, Irene thought.

Sam continued to rant. "You've made our life a living hell, Irene. She's pregnant. Leave her alone."

"Please," she said, "it'll go on his permanent record."

"He deserves to have a record," Sam shouted. "He's a criminal."

Arthur had reached them by then. "Now, Sam, let's cool it, okay?"

Sam eyed Arthur, and to Irene, it seemed something passed between them. "You know this is wrong, Arthur," Sam said.

Arthur nodded. "Yes, but . . ."

Antigone grabbed Sam's sleeve. "Sam." He immediately turned to his wife.

"Tigg, he beat the crap out of Ryder and hurt this poor animal, just for kicks."

When Antigone tilted her head up to her husband, Irene saw that her cheeks were moist with tears. Still she stroked the deer. And when she turned her eyes toward Irene, Irene felt uncomfortable. She told herself that she had done nothing wrong. Boys will be boys, as Arthur said. How she hated that excuse when Arthur used it, but this was her son, her first born, facing jail.

"Where does it end, Irene?" Antigone said.

"What?"

"This." Antigone swept her hand out in frustration. "You brought this on."

"I'm just trying to be a good mother, Antigone."

"And what is a good mother, Irene?" Antigone asked. "Does she bake cookies? Does she read to her kids every night? Does she bail them out of jail?"

"He's wild, I know," Irene said, glancing back at Art Junior. "But . . ."

"Where does it end? There will always be another book you don't like, Irene."

Irene turned back to Antigone, giving the lapel of her black wool coat a tug. "I've always tried to do the right thing, Antigone. To set an example."

Antigone shook her head, as if she didn't know whether to laugh or cry. "You're a handful, Irene."

Irene was surprised she wasn't more insulted. "I was raised that way," she said.

Antigone turned back to the deer, her hand still stroking. "A good mother doesn't give up," Antigone said softly.

"If I could just take him home—" Irene swallowed then pulled herself together. "We will deal with this, as a family."

In a tired voice, Antigone said to Cody, "Let them go," and Irene shut her eyes. A reprieve. When she opened them, she realized she'd been dismissed. Bent over the deer, Antigone was no longer interested in her. She started to say thank you, then noticed Antigone's shoulders shaking.

Arthur tugged at her elbow. Together they stumbled back to the gate.

As Cody removed the cuffs, Arthur ordered their son into the car. "You're grounded," he said.

"You gotta be kidding," Art Junior grumbled. "And look what they did to my Jeep."

"Don't worry about it," Arthur said. "It's not yours anymore."

THE VET AND SAM cut the fence to free Fancy. Then the vet gave the deer a shot for pain and another to relax her. Together Sam, Ryder, and the vet supported the deer as it staggered a step or two, then collapsed on the ground. Finally, after stitching up the deer's leg and jaw, the vet stood and wiped his hands on a towel from his gear, "There's not much more I can do, Antigone. She's lost a lot of blood."

After the vet left, Sam hunkered down beside Antigone and begged her to come inside, "It's freezing out here. You're exhausted."

"No," said Antigone, "I'm staying with her." She was sitting on the ground, the deer's bloody head in her lap. She stroked Fancy and whispered to her. Sam sat down beside her. Ryder jammed his hands in his pockets and stood nearby, as did Earthly and Star. Earthly put her arm around Star. William handed out hot chocolate from a thermos then took up a position by the front gate, pacing.

The vigil lasted through the rest of the night. As dawn finally spread across the winter sky, Fancy pushed her snout into Antigone's hand and blew one last time. Antigone felt the deer's last warm breath float away. She leaned over and whispered, "Good-bye, baby."

Star turned into her mother's arms and began to cry. Sam helped Antigone struggle to her feet. Her legs buckled, pinpricks of feeling rushing into her legs after sitting for hours at the deer's side. She clutched Sam's shirt. He tucked her head under his chin and held her close while she sobbed. Earthly shepherded Star home, and William returned to his apartment over the café. Ryder stood to the side, fists still in his pockets, looking at the ground.

Finally, Antigone straightened, wiped her face, and said, "Take care of her, Sam." He nodded. "Someplace nice. By the pond. She liked the pond." Then Antigone walked alone across the yard, through the gate, and into the house.

A few minutes later as Sam was talking to Ryder about burying the deer, Antigone came back out with car keys in her hand, got into the Mustang, and sped away. She heard Sam calling her name. In the rearview mirror, she saw him and Ryder running after the car, but she couldn't stop. Somewhere, out there, was a road that would help her forget.

CHAPTER 25

THE PINK SHARK

A FURIOUS EARTHLY SIMS was a sight to behold. As her ex-husband Chester used to say before he went over to the dark side, "Righteous law do look good on you, woman." So did her fuchsia suit with matching high heels and big feathered hat. She hadn't been this mad since Chester sold out, turned corporate, and got that strip mining company off on a technicality. Her baby girl, crying her heart out over a dead deer, wouldn't get out of bed. Her friend and partner Antigone was God knew where. It was time somebody paid.

The meeting was being held on the stage in the Mercy High School Auditorium. The seven board members and Superintendent Bradford Mitchell were seated on one side of a long table; Earthly stood on the other side. The *Mercy Full* frieze danced behind her. She gave the board her best shark smile and thought she saw Superintendent Mitchell gulp.

"Ladies and gentlemen, I graduated at the top of my class at Tulane. I had one of the best litigation records during my eleven years with the ACLU. In short, you are not the first school board I have faced. When I was actively practicing and not selling fine outlet linen, I sued school districts for discrimination, denial of civil rights and religious freedom, and even book banning."

"Now, see here . . ." said old Howard, the hardware store owner.

Earthly ignored him. "And when I sue someone, they don't forget it."

Superintendent Mitchell said, "Ms. Sims, this whole situation has been blown out of proportion."

"You bet it has. Banning books without a review . . ."

"This school board had nothing to do with that," said Hank the accountant, casting a furious glance at Irene.

"Refusing to return the books to circulation—even after said books had been reviewed and deemed suitable for students." Several members of the board glared at the superintendent.

"Persecuting an innocent woman, her family, and her business."

"There is such a thing as community standards . . ." interrupted Irene.

"Shut up, Irene," Hank growled.

Earthly continued, "You even got my client arrested on obscenity charges. A pregnant woman spent a night in jail."

"Now that wasn't our fault," said Gary the dentist.

"Oh, no, none of us would ever want that," said Kalinda the artist.

"We have no control over the county prosecutor," said Hank. "That had nothing to do with us."

Earthly pulled out a chair, sat down, and shuffled the papers in front of her. "I've already taken care of Mr. Braxton Richey," Earthly said, looking up with an evil smile. "And now I'm going to take care of you."

Ellen, who volunteered at the food pantry and various other nonprofits in town, said, "What do you mean?"

Earthly studied the woman who was pleasant, often shopped at The Great Cover Up, and dressed like a walking gunny sack. "Ellen, someone has to pay for this disruption to my client's life, not to mention the stress at a critical time in her pregnancy."

"There was no personal vendetta against Antigone," Irene insisted. "We're simply looking after our children. As is our right."

"You can restrict what you or your children read, Irene, but you cannot call upon other governmental or public agencies to do your dirty work."

"That's absurd," Irene smacked her hand on the table. "We support this school and library with our taxes."

"Nevertheless," Earthly said, "The First Amendment is clear. No government may prohibit the expression of an idea simply because society finds the idea itself offensive or disagreeable. That's the Supreme Court's opinion and the law of the land."

"Well, I don't like it." Irene tossed her head.

Hank cleared his throat. "Enough. What's it going to take to settle this matter, Earthly?"

"Yeah," said Luther, the mill foreman. "How much?"

"Two million." Earthly studied the group. "Per board member. And $3 million from the district." Silence.

Ellen's jaw dropped.

"Denial of civil rights doesn't come cheap," Earthly said. "We're not talking about a towel with an uneven hem."

"You're nuts!" erupted Luther.

Earthly leaned her hands on the table and stared each board member in the eye. She said firmly, "If I don't get what I want, this little stunt is going to cost you. And you can bet that this will not be a quiet lawsuit."

Gary, the chamber president, groaned.

The fingers gripping Irene's jacket were nearly white. "What do you really want?"

"To make this all go away?" Earthly asked.

Irene gave a curt nod.

"ALL the books back in circulation. Today."

CHAPTER 26

THEY WENT WHICHA WAY?

ANTIGONE HAD BEEN GONE for nearly eight hours. Sam and Ryder sat in silence at the kitchen table, jumping each time the phone rang. Between them, a box of Froot Loops lay on its side, its colorful contents pouring onto the table. Every once in a while one of them would mindlessly pluck a handful of cereal from the pile and pop it into his mouth. They'd long ago alerted the authorities, the highway patrol, but it was as if Antigone had driven that little red Mustang straight into a black hole.

It was four in the afternoon when there was a knock on the front door. Sam answered and found a boy on the front porch. Ryder joined him and frowned. "Stanley? I told you not to keep bringing this crap to our door."

"It's not a book," said the scrawny boy, shoving his red

hair out of his eyes. "It's for the deer lady." And then he thrust a piece of folded paper in Sam's hand, turned, and sprinted away. Sam unfolded the loose leaf sheet. It was a crayon drawing of what he assumed were supposed to be Antigone and her deer. The stick figures frolicked under a sun shining big and yellow in the corner of the page. It said, "Sorry about your dead deer." On the doorstep were other notes and cards, all addressed to the "Library Lady" or the "Deer Lady."

Sam peered across the road, where a memorial of flowers, stuffed animals, toys, and candles was growing near the gate to the O. Henry Deer Farm.

ANTIGONE'S CALL CAME AT 2:13 a.m. on Friday, eighteen hours after she'd sped out of Mercy. A startled Sam fell out of the chair where he'd been dozing as he leaped for the phone. Digging through the cards and papers, he scrambled for the phone.

"Hello. Hello. Don't hang up. I'm here."

"Sam?"

"Tigg? Where are you?"

"Sam, I need you."

Sam pushed his hands through his hair and realized they were shaking. "Where are you?"

"I don't know. It's snowing, and there aren't any signs. It's dark. I need you, Sam."

"Okay, stay calm." Sam mumbled to himself, "Think, think."

"Sam?"

"Don't worry, honey."

"Sam, I think the baby's coming. I can't drive anymore."

"It's too early, Tigg."

"I know. I keep telling the baby that, but she's not listening to me. This is definitely your child, Sam Thorne."

"Let's stay calm."

"I am calm, as calm as I'm going to get," she said with a moan.

"Look, Tigg, I'm coming to get you. Describe where you are."

Sam knew by the silence that she was trying to recall roads and landmarks. He waited, then began scribbling notes on the back of a crumpled envelope as she began to talk. "Tennessee. I peed at the welcome center. Left the interstate. Needed a nap. Two-lane roads. Mountains. I passed a town; I don't know how long ago."

"Think, honey."

"There was a billboard for a ski area."

Sam tried to keep his voice calm. "Good. What else?"

"I think I'm in a roadside park. Fell asleep. Don't know how long ago. It's snowing." Antigone cried out.

"Tigg!"

"Sam! The pains are coming."

"Like regularly?"

"Like this kid is kick boxing in my uterus."

"I'm calling the highway patrol. And then I'm coming after you."

"How? You'll never find me."

"I've got the GPS."

Ryder leaned over his shoulder and read his scribbles. "I'm coming along."

Sam put his hand over the receiver. "I can do this."

Ryder crossed his arms over his chest. "You're not leaving me behind."

Sam didn't want to take the time to fight. "Fine." He said to Antigone, "I'm bringing Ryder."

"Is that a good idea? You two are like Siamese fighting fish." Antigone gasped in pain, and Sam wanted to fling the telephone against the wall. "Don't kill each other before you get here," she said.

"We'll manage. Thank God, you had the cell phone with you this time. Promise you'll keep in touch."

"Promise." There was a pause. "But hurry."

RYDER GATHERED BLANKETS, COATS, and flashlights. William handed him a thermos of coffee and a bag of food. He smacked Sam on the shoulder. "Take it easy. Keep a cool head. Bring her back."

With a wave, Sam and Ryder drove off in Sam's truck. Sam got half way down the road, realized he was going the wrong way and turned around. They waved again.

"We shoulda got more veggie burgers," Ryder said, watching a waving William pass by the window. "This could take longer than I thought."

When the cell phone went silent in the middle of a conversation with Antigone, both Ryder and Sam panicked. One minute she was talking to them, and then nothing. Ryder reported the phone was dead, and they'd forgotten the adapter.

No phone. No GPS. "Find me a town," Sam shouted, pointing to the glove box. "Map."

Ryder hunched over the map of Tennessee. "What exactly are we looking for?"

"An electronics store."

"At this time of day?" Ryder glanced out the window. It was five in the morning.

They found a town, and then they found Crazy Jerry's Electronic City: 24 Hours of Plugged In, Amped Up, Out-a-sight Online Fun. Ryder and Sam scrambled out of the truck and ran to the store entrance. Even at this time of morning, Crazy Jerry's was hopping.

In Crazy Jerry's, Ryder and Sam leapt over the remote-controlled hot rod barreling down on them, fishtailed around a kid tapping on a computer terminal, and skidded to a stop in front of a wall of circuits, sockets, plugs, cords, antennas, and adapters.

Sam grabbed two packets and dashed for the register. He slammed a package of batteries and a phone adapter on the counter. The teenager behind the register smiled at him, "I hope you found everything to your satisfaction at Crazy Jerry's. We're crazy to please." The clerk tapped on the computer in front of him. "May I have your area code please?"

"I don't have a phone," Sam said, digging in a back pocket for his wallet.

The clerk looked pointedly at the phone adapter. "Your zip code then, sir?"

"I don't have one of those either," Sam said, throwing two twenty dollar bills on the counter. "That'll cover it."

"But, sir," the clerk looked frantic. "I only need a little information for our records."

"I don't have any information," Sam shouted, pulling Ryder out of the store.

As Ryder plugged in the adapter, Sam muttered, "God, I hate people who need to know everything about you." He threw the truck into gear with a squeal of rubber and immediately took a wrong turn out of the mall.

"Same here," Ryder said, beginning to notice the unfamiliarity of the road. "Didn't we cross railroad tracks and pass a taxidermy shop on the way into town? Where's the sign with the deer head? Uh, Sam, I think we're going the wrong way."

"You've got the goddamn GPS," Sam said. "Find out where the hell we are."

Ryder located their coordinates and got Sam driving in the general direction of Antigone. Again.

CHAPTER 27

THE SUNSET IS NOT AS CLOSE AS IT SEEMS

THIS USED TO BE easier, Antigone thought. Once riding into the sunset had been a cinch. It had occurred to her in the last few hours that all the heroes who rode off into the sunset—the masked men, the cowboys, the private eyes on Route 66—had never suffered a single labor pain. No wonder they were so happy and mobile.

This had been the most miserable road trip she could recall. Her sense of direction was on the fritz again, probably thanks to baby hormones. She had no idea where she was. And she had the awful feeling that she had been going in circles. She could be just a few hours from her own backyard in North Carolina and not know it. Several times she had pulled over on some back road and taken a nap. Her back ached, her feet were falling asleep, and her bladder kept demanding that she stop and shuffle off behind some tree. As she got back in the car one more time, she thought, "This is why I don't go camping."

She sought the old feelings she usually met on the road, the feelings of freedom and adventure and forgetfulness. But on this trip, no dotted lines, no voices on the radio, could distract her. She still saw Fancy in her mind, still felt life leaving the deer in an exhausted huff. She could not forget the mess her life was in—alone, on the side of the road, with a child anxious to come and no hospital, or husband, in sight.

A pain corkscrewed up her middle, turning her inside out. Antigone bit her lip. She tried to remember how the perky Lamaze teacher told them to breathe. She tried Sam again, and this time someone answered. "Where the hell have you been?" she cried.

"Sorry, technical difficulties," Sam said. "You okay?"

"Talk to me," she begged.

She pushed her back against the corner of the Mustang's backseat, stretched her legs across it, and listened to Sam's comforting voice. She followed his words through the twisting trails of pain, grasping on for dear life to images and moments they had shared. "Remember that time at the beach," he said. "That sand crab attacked me, and the pelicans . . ."

"No birds, pelicans or storks," she grunted.

"Okay, okay, breathe. In and out like with the waves."

"I can't do this. I don't want to do this anymore."

"Hang on, honey. I'm coming. Breathe, Tigg, just breathe."

On and on Sam talked and she listened, the phone on the floor beside her on speaker, both hands clutching the seat with white knuckles. She gritted her teeth. "Don't fight it," the Lamaze teacher had told them. Fight? Someone give her a white flag; she was ready to surrender. Only Sam's voice was real, her only strength, and she clung to it.

More than once Antigone thought she was going to die that night. She thought the pain would just carry her away, and she would never see Sam or Ryder again; she'd never get to meet her baby. She was going to die, she sobbed, and so she made promises to the universe.

"I'll be a good girl. I'll stop stirring up trouble. No more binge driving. No more talk radio shows. I'll be the perfect mother. I'll bake cookies and make things with craft paper and pipe cleaners. I'll be nicer to everyone—even Irene. I'll even close the library, if only you'll keep my baby safe . . ."

Sam and the highway patrol reached Antigone at the same time. It was close to 7:00 a.m., and the sun was struggling to punch its way through the overcast sky. The officer took one look at Antigone, radioed for paramedics, and announced, "This baby's not going to wait."

"No kidding," Antigone cried.

"It's too soon," Sam said.

"Not according to this little one," said the officer.

And so, Antigone, Sam, Ryder, and a highway patrol officer named Ginelli brought into the world a perfect baby girl in the backseat of a red Mustang convertible. Ginelli, with seven children of his own, was an expert and calmly directed operations. When it was done and Antigone and baby were each wrapped in crackling space blankets scavenged from Ginelli's emergency kit, Sam turned to Ryder and said, "Well, that involved more blood and screaming than I ever want to see or hear again."

"I'm with you," Ryder said.

Sometime, during the hollering and panting, the skies had cleared and the snow had stopped. Outside the sun was bright, glistening on the snow-covered hills. Inside the car, bundled in the backseat next to Sam, an exhausted Antigone watched Ryder instruct her husband on how to hold his new daughter.

"You gotta support her head. Like this." Ryder leaned in through the window and positioned Sam's hands.

Sam cupped the baby's head with his big hands. It was amazing, Antigone thought, that their daughter was almost exactly a handful, fitting nicely into her father's palm.

"There's nothing to her. I'm afraid I'll crush her," Sam said.

"First-time fathers," Officer Ginelli laughed.

Sam's cell phone rang. Ryder reached into Sam's shirt pocket and retrieved it. It was William.

"Everything okay?"

"Yeah, if Sam can figure out how to hold a baby," Ryder said. "It's a girl. Star nailed it—as usual."

IRENE STRODE THROUGH THE door of the O. Henry Café just as William stabbed the off button on his cell phone and hollered, "It's a girl! Oolong tea on the house!"

She glanced around the restaurant. The place was packed. She spotted Star and Earthly in a booth.

"I knew it," Star said, jumping out of the booth and whirling around in a circle.

"How's Antigone?" Earthly asked.

William pulled up. "Oh, I don't know!"

Earthly sighed, "Men."

"She must be all right," William stammered. "I mean Ryder would have told me if something was wrong, wouldn't he?"

"Probably," Irene said, clutching her purse and walking over to an empty stool at the counter.

As she passed Earthly's booth, she said, "I can be here if I want."

"It's a free country, Irene." Earthly smiled.

William offered Irene a cup of tea. She made a face and ordered coffee, black. She didn't know why she was here. For some reason, when she got up this morning, she'd felt this need to be at the restaurant. She sipped her coffee, listening to people worry about Antigone and discuss the recent events in Mercy. After one glance, she avoided looking at the door leading to Antigone's library. Bookhenge, she thought with disgust, what kind of name is that for a library?

Exchanging another look with Earthly, who nodded and smiled again, Irene wondered why she wasn't more upset. On Monday morning, those awful books would be back on the shelves in the Mercy High School Media Center. Maybe it was the phone call she'd intercepted this morning. It was the Japanese couple calling again, asking for Arthur. Irene had looked right across the breakfast table at her husband and said, "He's not here, and we aren't interested in selling the house."

Arthur didn't say a word.

And now there was a new child in Mercy. It had been quite a morning, Irene thought. She took a sip of her coffee and almost smiled.

WAITING FOR THE AMBULANCE to arrive to take his wife and child to the nearest hospital, Sam watched Tigg drift off toward sleep. Just as she was about to enter the place of dreams, she jerked awake and mumbled, "Sam?"

Sam leaned over and gently stroked his wife's damp hair. He adjusted the extra coats they'd bundled under Antigone's head for a pillow.

"What?" he whispered.

"I made some promises."

"I heard. The speaker phone was working just fine. You were yelling loud enough for my mom to hear you in Florida."

"I promised to give up the library."

"You also promised to be nicer to Irene. Like that's going to happen."

"But about the library . . ."

Sam personally thought pledges made in the throes of labor—while another human being was trying to crawl out of you head first—didn't count. Now was not the time to say so, though.

"Our daughter's going to need good books to read to her mother," he said, looking down at the tiny, sleeping babe cradled protectively inside his jacket. He heart was so full he was amazed it didn't just explode from his chest.

Antigone smiled. "Yes, she is." And then Sam watched utter exhaustion overtake his wife, just as he had the very first time they met. He'd touched her cheek then, too, while she was asleep and wouldn't remember. That day, he'd sat on the trunk of the Mustang, inexplicably happy, watching over her. And he'd felt a lightness, the world coming into balance— just like now.

ACKNOWLEDGMENTS

THIS BOOK WAS MANY years in its making. It lost its fire for a while, then my daughter came home from high school with a disturbing report, "They're banning books," and the embers were re-ignited. Suddenly, my ideals as a writer ran smack against my protectiveness as a parent. I watched censorship challenge individual freedoms in our North Carolina town, cause a beloved teacher to resign, and prompt many of us to examine the sides we take in such conflicts.

According to the American Library Association, on average about five hundred books are challenged every year in the United States—and those are just the ones we know about. Some would say this is horrible. But I think if we didn't have a way to challenge the actions of others, we wouldn't be truly free. So I accept that book challenges are necessary, but I also am happy when they fail.

I would like to thank those who have so generously given me their time, attention, and wisdom while writing this book: Marlys Dooley, Lois West Duffy, Miriam Karmel, Janet Hanafin, Jean Housh, Connie Szarke,

Ann Woodbeck, and our talented leader, Faith Sullivan. You have made me an infinitely better writer. I am in awe of your work and feel so lucky to have you.

Thank you also to several mentors: Barbara Graybeal, who has always been a keen supporter and smart editor; Ellen Hart, who is unfailingly kind, a wonderful writer, and the first person to introduce me to Dennis LeHane's books; Mary Carroll Moore, who gave me detailed and excellent advice; and sculptor Jim Gallucci, who let me weld with him for a day.

To Suzanne Roberts and Sarah Roberts Delacueva, thank you for your love and energy, which brighten my every day. Also, I am grateful to Sarah for editing this book not once, but twice, and stunning me each time with her intelligent observations (and good catches). Finally, and most importantly, thank you to Tony—you never give up on me, never stop trying to inspire me, and never let me rest too long. Yes, I know there is always another mountain, and you are waiting for me, hand outstretched, ready to help me climb it. I'm there with you until the end of time.

ABOUT THE AUTHOR

SHERRY ROBERTS IS THE author of award-winning mysteries and literary fiction. *Down Dog Diary* and *Warrior's Revenge* are part of the Maya Skye novels. *Book of Mercy* is a funny novel about a serious issue: censorship, *Maud's House* is a story of lost-and-found creativity, and *WriteTips* is a guide to giving your writing power and improving your business.

She has contributed essays and articles to national publications and anthologies including *USA Today* and the *Saint Paul Almanac.* Her short fiction has been published in newspapers, literary magazines, and *O. Henry Literary Festival Short Stories.*

She lives in Apple Valley, Minnesota, where she feeds the hummingbirds, rides her bike, reads by the fire, bakes cookies, and practices yoga and tai chi.

Visit Sherry's website at sherry-roberts.com.

WHAT'S NEXT?

SIGN UP FOR SHERRY'S EMAIL LIST (sherry-roberts.com) for updates on future writing—plus get free books, short stories, or other offers available only to fans! Your email will never be shared, you can unsubscribe at any time, and Sherry promises not to paper your inbox with emails.

Also follow Sherry Roberts Author on Facebook to get the latest on her books and writing in general.

LEAVE A REVIEW. If you enjoyed this book, please consider leaving a brief review on Goodreads, Amazon, or other retailer site. Readers spreading the word to other readers is invaluable to authors and their work. If you're shy, just drop me a line on the contact page of sherry-roberts.com. Your support and ideas are important to me. I promise I'll write back.

CHECK OUT MY OTHER BOOKS. In *Down Dog Diary*, yoga teacher Maya Skye goes up against killers to protect a mysterious diary. In *Warrior's Revenge*, she faces an opponent not only bent on revenge—but murder. In *Maud's House*, an artist loses her creativity but finds love. All of my books are available in paperback and eBook at sherry-roberts.com, Amazon, and other retail outlets. If you can't find my books in your local bookstore, ask for them. Ask your local library to carry my books.

www.ingramcontent.com/pod-product-compliance
Lightning Source LLC
Chambersburg PA
CBHW020759250626
47155CB00003B/1149